NO PAIN, N

"All right, girls," Lugo said.
Who wants to go first?"

"I'll start," Harry said. "But I'm still working on putting all the elements together. I'll show you what I've done so far."

"No!" Lugo said. "Do you know how to do the hecht or not?"

"Well, yes," Harry said. "I know *how*. But I haven't—"

"Then do it." Lugo pointed at the uneven bars. "Now."

Taking a deep breath, Harry jumped up to grab the top bar. She started swinging higher and harder, until her body was bumping the lower bar on the downswing.

Then, when the momentum felt right, she swung hard, let go, and curled around the lower bar. Suddenly she panicked, but there was nothing to hold on to. She had to follow through. Feeling frightened, she let her body circle the lower bar. The momentum took her up and out. Instinctively she stretched her arms overhead and got ready to land feetfirst. Almost before she knew it, her feet slapped against the crash mat. Automatically she assumed the "touchdown" position.

Lugo looked satisfied. "There, you see? You did it. We'll work on technique later. Remember that fear is a useless emotion. It's for babies. You want a big result, you make a big try. Okay, who's next?"

Be sure to read all the exciting
AMERICAN GOLD GYMNASTS
titles from Bantam Books:

#1 Competition Fever
#2 Balancing Act
#3 Split Decision
#4 The Bully Coach

by Gabrielle Charbonnet

The Bully Coach

BANTAM BOOKS
NEW YORK • TORONTO • LONDON • SYDNEY • AUCKLAND

RL 5, 008–012

THE BULLY COACH

A Bantam Skylark Book / August 1996

Skylark Books is a registered trademark of Bantam Books, a division of Bantam Doubleday Dell Publishing Group, Inc. Registered in U.S. Patent and Trademark Office and elsewhere.

Series design: Madalina Stefan

ISBN 0-553-48299-8

Published simultaneously in the United States and Canada.

Bantam Books are published by Bantam Books, a division of Bantam Doubleday Dell Publishing Group, Inc. Its trademark, consisting of the words "Bantam Books" and the portrayal of a rooster, is Registered in U.S. Patent and Trademark Office and in other countries. Marca Registrada. Bantam Books, 1540 Broadway, New York, New York 10036.

PRINTED IN THE UNITED STATES OF AMERICA

OPM 0 9 8 7 6 5 4 3 2 1

The Bully Coach

Chapter One

"Did you guys see Elena Berrish last night?" Kelly Reynolds asked her fellow Silver Stars. "Talk about awesome."

"She's got to be a contender for a medal," Kelly's best friend, Monica Hales, said.

"I'm predicting at least a bronze for the uneven bars," said Kathryn Stiles.

The three girls crossed the huge open gym of Sugarloaf Gymnastic Academy, the gymnastic training center that Kelly's mother, Emma Stanton, owned. As usual, it was a crowded and busy Saturday morning, with two different groups—the Silver Stars and the Gold Stars—working on their gymnastics.

"She deserves a silver," Kelly said. "Or maybe an all-around medal."

"Hey, are you guys talking about the compulsories on TV last night?" Hiroko "Harry" Kobayashi, another Silver Star, joined her teammates as they headed for the gym's uneven parallel bars.

"What else?" Monica answered.

Kelly grinned. Since the Olympic Games had begun two weeks before, she and the five other Silver Stars had talked about practically nothing else. Not only were the games taking place in their very own hometown, Atlanta, but in the past few days the gymnastics competition had begun. It was the television event of the year.

"Okay, Silvers, let's go," Emma Stanton called. "Have you guys warmed up?"

"Yes, Emma," Kelly said. At home she called her mother Mom, but at SGA she called her Emma like the other students.

"Is everyone here?" Emma glanced around, looking for all six Silver Stars.

At Sugarloaf Gymnastic Academy, students were divided into teams based on age and ability. The youngest were the Twinklers, who were four and five years old. Students fourteen years old and older were Gold Stars. They were an elite group, most of them aiming for the Olympics. Between the Twinklers and the Gold Stars were the Copper Stars, Bronze Stars, and Silver Stars. These teams were for the best students in their age groups.

Kelly, Monica Hales, and Kelly's stepsister,

Maya Resnikov, were all twelve-year-old Silver Stars. The three other members of their team, the twins Kathryn and Candace Stiles and Harry Kobayashi, were eleven. As Silver Stars, they had class every Tuesday, Wednesday, and Thursday afternoon, and Saturday morning.

Besides Emma, Dimitri Resnikov was their other main coach. Almost four months earlier, Dimitri and his daughter, Maya, had moved to America from Russia. Dimitri and Emma had gotten married, and now the four of them lived in a big Victorian house not too far from SGA. It had been a major adjustment for Kelly, suddenly having a stepfather and a stepsister, but now she could hardly remember what it had been like when it had been just her and Emma.

"Let's see . . ." Emma consulted her clipboard. "Today we're going to start learning a new dismount for the uneven bars, then Dimitri has an announcement to make, then maybe you can work on your floor routines with Susan." Susan Lu was their assistant coach. She had been a world-class gymnast until a few years earlier, when she had injured herself too badly to compete again. The Silvers called her General Lu sometimes, because she was so strict about following all the safety rules.

Emma put down her clipboard and rested one

hand on the lower bar. "I'd like to lead Harry through this dismount first," she said. "We'll take it step by step, then put the steps together. Okay, Harry. You need to start in a monkey swing from the high bar."

With Emma's help, Harry jumped up to hang from the top bar of the apparatus. Harry was Japanese American and the smallest of the Silver Stars. Today her shiny black hair was in a short, bouncy ponytail, held in place with a pale pink scrunchie that matched her sleeveless unitard.

"Now, to perform a hecht dismount," Emma continued, "Harry will do a couple of big monkey swings, building momentum and bumping her hips against the lower bar. Then she'll release her hands, curling her body around the lower bar in a fast hip circle. If she has enough power going, she'll release from the lower bar like so"—Emma demonstrated with her hands—"and fly over it in a swan dive. Then her feet will point floorward and she'll have a regular landing here on the crash mat."

Kelly nodded. She had seen the hecht dismount performed hundreds of times—by the Gold Stars and by professional gymnasts on television and at meets.

"This is a great-looking dismount," Maya whispered to her.

"Yeah, I can't wait to try it," Kelly answered,

thinking again how lucky she was that her stepsister loved gymnastics as much as she did. It gave them a huge thing in common and had made it easier to become a family.

"Now, when it feels right, Harry," Emma said, "release your hands and let the momentum carry you under and around the lower bar in a hands-free hip circle."

"Okay." Harry swung again, going higher each time and bouncing her hips against the lower bar. With Emma spotting her, she suddenly let go of the top bar and piked her legs, bending sharply at her hips with her knees straight and together. With her body curled, she circled the lower bar, ending up balanced on top of it, her legs straight and her hands out to the sides.

"Excellent," Emma said. "That was terrific. We'll practice this move until you're completely comfortable with it. Who wants to be next?" She leaned against the lower bar, rubbing her forehead.

"I'll go next," said Kathryn. She and Harry both liked the uneven bars the best. Kelly and Maya preferred the balance beam; Monica was best on the vault, and Candace always loved doing floor work.

"Um, okay," Emma said distractedly, passing her hand over her eyes. She frowned.

"Emma, are you okay?" Maya asked.

Kelly went over to her mother. "Mom, are you all right? You suddenly look kind of . . . green."

"I'm okay," Emma murmured, smiling weakly. "I guess I'm just hungry." She put her hand to her mouth and frowned. "Can you guys excuse me?" she said. "I'll be right back. Do some more stretching exercises." She turned and walked quickly to the girls' rest room at the back of the gym.

"Should I go after her?" Kelly asked Maya.

Her stepsister shook her head. "She might want to be alone."

"What's the matter with her?" Candace asked. "Does she have a stomach bug or something?"

"I don't know," Kelly said with a shrug. "Maybe she's coming down with the flu."

"Do *you* feel okay?" Maya asked tentatively.

"Yeah, why?" Kelly met Maya's eyes.

"It's just that, you know, you made chili last night," Maya said.

While Monica and the others giggled, Kelly put her hands on her hips. "Maya, my chili was perfectly fine! I followed all the directions and everything. Are you saying my cooking made Mom sick?"

"No, no," Maya said hastily. "I just, you know, wondered."

"Well, quit wondering," Kelly said. "I'm not

sick, and you're not sick, and Dimitri's not sick, and we all ate my chili. Something else is wrong with Mom, okay?"

"Yeah, okay," Maya said, smothering a giggle.

"Sorry, girls," Emma said cheerfully, coming back from the rest room. "I just needed to splash some water on my face. Now, Kathryn, do you want to try the hecht dismount?"

"Sure." Kathryn climbed to the top bar and hung by her arms. She swung several times, then released her hands and curled her body around the lower bar. Catching herself on the bar, she balanced there, waiting for Emma's next instruction.

"Great, Kathryn, excellent try," Emma said. "Let's take a five-minute water break; then the rest of you can try it."

Kathryn jumped down from the bar, and she and Harry slapped high fives.

As Emma led the way to the water fountain, Kelly raised her eyebrows at Maya. Her mother seemed to be fine now. One thing was for sure: It *hadn't* been her chili!

Chapter Two

Monica took a quick sip of water, then stepped back to make room for Kathryn. Almost automatically she scanned the gym for the light of her life, Beau Jarrett. Beau was a Gold Star and totally out of her league—he was sixteen and in high school—but she'd had a killer crush on him for at least six months.

"He's not here yet," Maya said, drinking from the fountain.

Monica blushed. "Who?" she asked, trying to sound casual.

"Beau Jarrett!" her fellow Silver Stars cried in unison.

Feeling as though her face were on fire, Monica drank some water and quickly changed the subject. "I heard you got an A on that last English quiz," she said to Maya. "Good for you."

"Thanks," Maya said with a grin. "I guess all that tutoring paid off." Although Maya spoke English very well, she'd been having trouble keeping up with some of her classes at school. For the past month she'd had a private tutor helping her. "I have to admit, I sort of miss Michael Ashton," she added.

Monica giggled. "Your adorable high-school English coach? Well, you could always pretend to do badly again."

"No thanks," Maya said. "I'm glad to have my Monday and Friday afternoons free now. What about you? How are things at Fur, Feather, and Scale?"

Recently Monica had decided to branch out in her interests a little bit and had taken a part-time job at a veterinarian's office in the strip mall where SGA was.

"Great, as usual," Monica said enthusiastically. "Did you know that Boston terriers almost always have to have cesarean sections when they have puppies? Their heads have been bred to be kind of too big to come out the normal way."

Kathryn made a face. "Gee, thanks for sharing that with us, Monica. I've been wondering about that for years." She rolled her eyes.

Kelly laughed and patted Monica on the shoulder. "I guess Kathryn isn't as crazy about animals as you are."

"Guess not," Monica agreed. "*I* thought it was really interesting."

"Ew, ew, gross!" Candace cried suddenly, putting her hand to her throat.

Monica turned to look where Candace was staring. The gym's official rodent control officer, a gray tabby kitten named Sam Gordon Andrew, was trotting toward Monica. Something small, limp, and brown was hanging from his mouth. Stopping before Monica, the kitten dropped a dead mouse at her feet.

"Oh, yuck," Kelly said, turning away. "Totally disgusting."

"I'm getting out of here," Harry said.

"I'll go get Dimitri," said Kathryn, heading off quickly.

"You guys," Monica said. "Y'all are being so rude. Sam Gordon Andrew is just trying to be nice. He thinks he's giving me a present. Probably because I'm the one who takes care of him."

Leaning over, she petted Sam Gordon Andrew and scratched behind his ears. "My, what a nice . . . mouse," she crooned, trying not to look at it. "Thank you so much. I really appreciate it." It wasn't that she liked dead mice. But it was the thought that counted.

"You're such a good hunter," Monica added. Sam Gordon Andrew purred and rubbed against her legs. Silently Monica hoped he wasn't rubbing his mouse-breath mouth all over her. But she would never hurt his feelings by pushing him away.

"Look, Emma," Maya said as their coach walked up. "Sam Gordon Andrew caught a mouse."

Emma's brown eyes widened as she looked down at the limp form by Monica's feet. Then her face went pale, and she put her hand to her mouth. "Excuse me," she muttered. Turning, she dashed for the girls' rest room once again.

Kelly immediately looked at Maya. "It *wasn't* the chili," she insisted.

"What's this about a mouse?" Dimitri's deep voice asked from behind Monica. Kathryn was close on his heels. "Let me see."

"Sam Gordon Andrew caught a mouse, and Emma's barfing," Candace said.

For a moment Dimitri looked worried, and his eyes went to the door of the girls' rest room in the back of the gym. Then he kneeled down to take care of the business at hand.

"I'll scoop up the mouse with this piece of cardboard," he said. He patted the kitten firmly on the head. "Good cat! You are supposed to catch mice, and you catch mice. Good boy!"

Sam Gordon Andrew, ecstatic at the praise, dropped to the floor and writhed happily. Monica laughed and rubbed his tummy.

Dimitri stood up with the mouse folded into the piece of cardboard. "Come, girls," he said, motioning toward the front of the gym. "I have an announcement to make to the Silver and Gold Stars. But first, I will check on Emma."

"Just don't show her the mouse again," Kelly advised him.

Two minutes later Maya and the other Silvers headed for the front of the gym. Emma's and Dimitri's offices were there, along with the first aid room and a waiting area for parents. The Gold Stars joined them one by one. Maya looked at the Gold Stars disdainfully. Most of the Golds were snobby. Maya decided that when *she* was a Gold Star, she would go out of her way to be nice to all the other students—from Silvers on down to Twinklers.

"I wonder what Papa has to announce," Maya said to Harry. "Is it good news or bad news?"

"That's the thing," Harry said, nodding. "Either we're all in trouble, or else something fabulous is about to happen. You never know."

Dimitri walked up and stood at the front of SGA, clapping his hands for quiet.

Maya looked at her father, feeling proud. Back in Russia, Dimitri had been a world-famous gymnastics coach and had trained several Olympic medal winners. Then, two years earlier, he had renewed an old friendship with Emma Stanton. Emma had been divorced when Kelly was only two years old, and they never saw Kelly's father. Maya's mother had died when Maya was seven. When Dimitri and Emma met again, they were both coaching gymnasts at a world championship meet. It had been love at first sight. For two years they had dated long distance, and then they had decided to get married.

It had been very hard for Maya at first. She'd left so many things behind in Russia: her friends, her gym, a lot of her belongings, and, most important, her grandmother. But now, after almost four months in the States, she felt that things were working out. She and Kelly got along well, and Emma was warm and caring. Maya had found a lot to like about America, too: the clothes, the food, television, the variety of people, the land. It was a special place, and she was glad she lived in it.

"As you all know," Dimitri began, "we've had many new students join Sugarloaf Gynmastic Academy in the last several months."

Maya nodded. Some of the new students had joined specially to train with her father.

"We've been interviewing coaches for the past few weeks—some of you may have met them," Dimitri went on.

Thinking back, Maya remembered two recent

tryouts: a male coach who'd barely known what he was doing, and a woman coach who'd been so nervous that she'd made everyone else twitchy too.

As Emma joined Dimitri at the front of the group, Maya glanced at her with concern. Emma was obviously feeling ill, but because SGA was busy with all the new students, Emma wasn't taking any days off.

"I'm happy to announce that we will soon have a guest coach whom I think you will all be pleased with," Dimitri said, smiling. "Lugo Bigue has recently terminated his contract with the Colorado High Flyers gym. As a favor to me, he has agreed to come and coach a two-week session here at SGA."

Gasping with delight, Maya turned to Harry. A huge smile was on Harry's face, and she held up a hand to slap high fives.

"Lugo Bigue!" Harry squealed happily. "Oh my gosh. He's only practically the most famous coach in the whole world, after Dimitri."

"It's like having Whitney Houston come give us singing lessons," Kelly said.

"This is incredible!" Kathryn said, bouncing excitedly. "I can't believe he's coming here."

Dimitri held up his hand for silence. "As you probably know," he continued, "Lugo coached Gail St. James and Galina Churovna for the Barcelona Olympics. Both of them won medals in 1992; Galina a silver for the uneven parallel bars. He's famous for producing winners. We're very glad that he's agreed to come help our own stable of winners."

"All right!" Kelly yelled, punching the air.

"Yes!" said Randi Marshall, a Gold Star.

Beau Jarrett and Paul Edinberg slapped high fives, and several of the other Golds were jumping up and down.

"Of course, we know everyone here will be on his or her best behavior," Dimitri said, pretending to frown critically at his audience. "We've decided Lugo's time will be best spent if he focuses on the Gold and Silver Stars. Emma, Susan, and I will concentrate on the other classes."

Emma stood next to Dimitri and smiled happily. Maya thought she looked better. Maybe she'd had a two-hour flu or something.

"Lugo will begin here next Tuesday," Emma announced. "He isn't coaching anyone in this year's Olympics. Are there any questions?"

No one had any questions. The students were too excited to think of anything to ask.

"This will be so great," Julie Stiller said to Randi. "I bet Lugo takes one look at me and decides to send me to the worlds."

Randi nodded in agreement. "He's supposed to

be incredible at spotting Olympic winners," she said.

Julie held her hands out. "Well, here I am!"

Randi laughed as she and Julie walked back to the floor mats.

Nearby, Maya and Kelly groaned at the same time.

"She's such a pain," Kelly said.

"With any luck, Lugo *will* want to send her to the worlds," Monica muttered. "*Another* world. Right away."

Maya laughed. Of all the snobby Golds, Julie Stiller was the snobbiest. She had started a feud with Maya and Kelly almost as soon as Maya had joined SGA, and it wasn't over yet. But Maya tried to put Julie out of her mind. The important thing was that Lugo Bigue was coming—and Maya would have to perform at her absolute best!

Chapter Three

"Do you have any plans for tomorrow?" Kelly asked Maya after dinner on Saturday night. They were downstairs in the family room, watching television. The evening's Olympic coverage included men's gymnastics.

Maya looked up from where she was slouched on the sofa.

"No," she answered. "Except I'll be practicing everything I know so I don't embarrass myself in front of Lugo Bigue on Tuesday."

Kelly snorted. "You couldn't embarrass yourself if you tried. You're practically good enough to be a Gold Star now. Lugo's going to think you're incredible."

Maya blushed, looking pleased. "He's supposed to be really tough," she said. "But everyone says he's technically brilliant. He can just look at you and know what you're doing wrong and how you need to fix it."

"We Silvers are tough enough to take anything he dishes out," Kelly said, flicking the volume down on the remote. "Oh, look, it's Alan Rivers. He's really good." She looked up. "You know, I think Lugo's coming is going to be a great thing. Sometimes a gymnast needs to change coaches to keep going forward. I bet Lugo will help us all improve. I definitely feel ready to go to the next level."

"Me too," Maya said. "Back in Russia, I knew a couple of girls who were chosen to be coached by him. I can remember how excited they were. I even knew Galina Churovna, before she left Russia and followed Lugo to Colorado."

"You did?" Kelly's eyes widened. "You never mentioned that before."

"I only knew her slightly," Maya said. "She was always working too hard to be that friendly. But I wasn't surprised when Lugo Bigue coached her to win a silver medal at the last Olympics. She was totally dedicated to gymnastics. Did nothing but work, work, work."

"Well, I'm ready to work, work, work too, if Lugo will help me get to the Olympics one day," Kelly said.

Crash! Kelly and Maya both jumped when they

heard the huge noise upstairs. For a moment they stared at each other in surprise; then they jumped up at the same time and headed for the stairs.

On the second floor, a cloud of dust was billowing out of the small room Dimitri and Emma used as an office.

Kelly skidded to a halt right outside the door. In another moment Emma and Dimitri stepped gingerly out of the doorway, waving their hands in front of their faces and coughing.

"What are you two doing?" Kelly demanded, putting her hands on her hips.

Emma smiled at her. "Oh, hi, sweetheart," she said. "We've decided to fix up this old office. Dimitri was just tapping the plaster walls to see if they needed patching."

"They do," Dimitri said. His eyes were glowing blue out of the powdered whiteness of his face.

"Papa," Maya groaned. "We just got the hallway fixed from where you tried to put up the bookcase. Now you've done it again!"

Dimitri looked guilty. "I just barely tapped the wall. And it's a good thing I did. What if the wall had suddenly fallen on someone? No, it's better to know now that it needs repair."

"Once he fixes the wall, we're going to paint the room and make new curtains," Emma said enthusiastically.

"But why?" Maya asked. "I thought the room was fine as your office."

Emma and Dimitri looked at each other, and Emma gave a tiny smile. "We just thought a change would be nice," she said.

Kelly and Maya looked at each other, their eyes narrowed suspiciously. Then Kelly shrugged.

"Why are they bothering?" Kelly asked as they headed back downstairs. "There are other rooms that need redoing more. Like mine, for example."

Maya giggled. "And mine. Who knows what they're up to? Let's just try to stay out of their way." She flopped back on the sofa.

"You got it. They're acting weird, with a capital *W*," Kelly said. "Parents—go figure."

Chapter Four

"I can't stand it," Maya panted on Tuesday afternoon as she and Kelly jogged down the sidewalk. "I want to get there *instantly.*" Sugarloaf Middle School, which all six Silver Stars attended, was only eight blocks from SGA. The girls often walked or rode their bikes to the gym after school.

"I know," Kelly said as they pounded along Peachtree Street. "I almost died when we had that last-minute assembly. It would have been just our luck to be kept late today of all days."

"One more block," Maya said. Her long blond hair streamed out behind her as she ran. Her backpack thumped heavily against her with every step.

"All right!" Kelly cheered breathlessly one block later. "Here we are!"

The two girls pushed through the double glass

doors of the gym and streaked to the girls' locker room in the back.

"Finally! Glad you decided to show up. I thought you two might be playing hooky," Monica teased, pretending to look at her watch. She'd obviously just gotten there herself, since she was still wearing her school clothes.

"Very funny," Maya panted, throwing down her backpack and pulling out her leotard. To impress Lugo Bigue, she had chosen to wear a traditional solid red, long-sleeved leotard, similar to ones she'd worn in competitions. She quickly changed into it, then pulled her hair into a tight braid, looping it up and out of the way with a scrunchie.

Without saying anything, she watched as her teammates prepared themselves to meet their new, important coach.

Kelly—unbelievably enough—was wearing a brand-new hot-pink unitard with short sleeves and legs that ended above her knees. It made a big change from her usual worn and ratty leotards.

"I'm so excited I can hardly get my hair in a ponytail," Harry muttered, pulling out her hair elastic and starting over. She was wearing a pale yellow short-sleeved leotard and looked cool and professional, as always.

Candace was in a turquoise bodysuit and matching biker shorts. Her twin, Kathryn, had on a sleek, shiny emerald-green leotard. It was clear that everyone wanted to impress Lugo. But it was Monica who was really going to make a splash. Maya grinned to herself as Monica hogged the mirror, trying to get her head scarf to cooperate. The tallest girl on their team and the only African American, she already stood out. But today she was wearing a vivid black-and-white zebra-print leotard with long sleeves. It dipped dramatically in the back, showing an expanse of creamy tan skin. Right now she was fussing with a red, green, and black scarf printed with a traditional African pattern. She had looped it around her puffy dark brown curls and was wrapping it across her forehead almost in a turban effect.

"You know, if we all do well today, maybe Lugo will want to stay here permanently," Kathryn said, taping her palms to protect them.

"That would be so incredible," Harry said.

"Yeah. If we had Emma, Dimitri, *and* Lugo, that would make SGA just about the most important gym in the country," Monica put in.

"So we Silvers know what we have to do, right?" Kelly asked, turning to face her teammates. "We have to knock Lugo's socks off!"

"That's right!" Maya cried, slapping high fives with Kelly.

Cheering happily, the Silver Stars roared out of the locker room and into the main part of the gym.

"Girls, Lugo is meeting the Gold Stars right now. Let's do some warm-ups, and then I'll bring him over to meet you," Dimitri said when the Silvers had gathered by the wall of mirrors.

Monica looked over at the Gold Stars as Dimitri led the Silvers in a thorough warm-up. Lugo Bigue was easy to pick out. Tall and muscular, he was blond like Dimitri, though his hair was straight and Dimitri's was curly. He had a neatly trimmed light brown mustache. His T-shirt was crisp and white, and his gray warm-up pants barely touched the tops of his clean white athletic shoes.

The Gold Stars seemed to be hanging on his every word, especially Killer Stiller, Monica noticed. Julie looked focused and determined, and Monica knew she would be pulling out all the stops in an attempt to impress Lugo. Beau Jarrett was there too. Monica sighed to herself as she stretched forward as far as she could and tried to touch her forehead to the ground. Beau was so adorable. Lugo didn't seem to be paying that much attention to him—maybe he was still getting to know the students. Then Lugo seemed to crack a joke; several of the Golds suddenly laughed, and their tension eased.

Monica stood with one foot poised on the barre that ran the length of the mirrors. Raising her arms gracefully overhead, she reached out and sideways in a balletic move that she hoped Beau was noticing. *Look at me,* she willed him mentally, but he seemed to be concentrating on what Lugo was saying.

Then the Silvers were warmed up, and Dimitri went to get the guest coach.

Monica shifted from one foot to another, feeling nervous and excited at the same time.

"I hope we like him," she whispered to Kelly.

"What's not to like?" Kelly whispered back, bouncing on her heels in anticipation. "He's practically the most famous coach in the world. His students are champions."

"Lugo Bigue, meet the Silver Stars," Dimitri said enthusiastically, drawing the new coach near. "You'll find them just as talented and dedicated as the Gold Stars."

Lugo Bigue smiled at each girl in turn. "I'm very pleased to meet you all," he said. He was Bulgarian; his English was more heavily accented than Dimitri's, Monica decided. "Dimitri has told me great things about you, and I'm very excited to have a chance to work with each of you. And where is your daughter, Dimitri? Which one is Maya?" His eyes wandered over the group.

"Here," Maya said shyly, stepping forward.

Lugo took both her hands in his, then turned to

smile at Dimitri. "The next generation, no? I am certain she will be a champion," he said.

Dimitri beamed proudly. "All of our gymnasts are very gifted."

"I am sure this one is *exceptionally* gifted," Lugo said, gazing at Maya approvingly. "She has the Resnikov blood."

From where she stood, Monica could see Maya blushing.

Gesturing to Kelly, Maya said, "That's my step-sister, Kelly Reynolds. Emma's daughter."

Lugo released Maya's hands, stepped over to Kelly, and took hers. Now Kelly blushed and looked at the ground.

"The daughter of the great Emma Stanton!" Lugo exclaimed. "What a privilege to be working with you. I'm sure I have little to teach you—you were probably born doing double saltos with a full twist."

"Oh, no, not really," Kelly muttered, a nervous smile on her face.

Monica crossed her arms over her chest and caught Kathryn's eye. Kathryn raised her eyebrows slightly. Monica guessed they were thinking the same thing. It was great that Lugo was so excited about working with Maya and Kelly, but there were four other Silver Stars too. As she watched Lugo gush over Maya and Kelly, Monica felt about as wanted as yesterday's dinner.

"Well!" Dimitri said cheerfully, rubbing his hands together. "I must go work with the Gold Stars. Lugo, perhaps you should get an idea of where the Silvers are in their training. Have them show you their stuff on the floor mats. And please call me if you need anything." With a wave, Dimitri left them and headed over to where Susan Lu was spotting the Gold Stars on the vault.

"Excellent," said Lugo, smiling at the Silvers. "Please, girls, I am anxious to see your talents. Maya Resnikov, would you go first? Give me your best floor routine."

In front of the large windows on the west wall, there was a flat, carpeted area forty feet by forty feet—the regulation size for a gymnastic floor routine. The Silvers lined up along one edge, and Maya walked to a corner, a look of concentration on her face.

Monica waited, wondering what Maya was going to do. Each girl had a personalized floor program that showed off her talents and helped conceal her weaknesses. Although Maya preferred working on the beam, Monica knew that her floor routine would be impressive.

Then Maya was running diagonally across the mat to build speed. When she was almost at the opposite corner, she threw herself into a high-speed walkover, popping down on her landing and bouncing back up with tremendous height and power. Using that momentum, she flipped backward into a back salto, landing again solidly, without even a wobble. Then she dropped into a straddle split, moving smoothly into a controlled handstand, then curling in again to a headstand and then a forward somersault.

Finally she stood and performed some dance movements, showing off her grace and natural flexibility. She ended with a back walkover and another back flip. After nailing that landing, she breathlessly threw her arms over her head in the traditional final gesture.

"Wow!" Kelly whispered to Monica as the Silvers broke into spontaneous applause.

Monica nodded, smiling broadly. It had been an incredible floor routine, especially since Maya hadn't had much warning before being asked to perform. "She looked fabulous," Monica whispered back.

Smiling modestly but looking pleased, Maya skipped lightly off the mats and came to stand by her teammates, waiting for Lugo's reaction.

Glancing at Lugo, Monica saw that he gave only a small nod.

"You achieved good height after your roundoff," he told Maya briskly. "And you have a lot of power. But your movements are often not crisp enough. It makes you look sloppy. Sometimes your line is flawed. And a gymnast your age should be doing more complicated skills."

Monica gaped at Lugo, as did her teammates. Maya looked as if she couldn't believe she had heard him correctly.

"Um," Maya said hesitantly, "Papa has been careful not to push me too far too fast. So I've been able to avoid serious injuries."

Lugo smiled. "Dimitri is a great, great coach," he said, some measure of his earlier friendliness resurfacing. "And I would never disagree with what he says. But sometimes one must take a small risk to achieve a big result, no?"

"I guess," Maya said, a tiny line appearing between her eyebrows.

Monica wasn't so sure Emma and Dimitri would agree with Lugo's thinking. But she was sure of one thing . . . the next two weeks were going to be very interesting.

Chapter Five

"The worst thing," Maya said that night at home as she and Kelly were starting to prepare dinner, "was that he was right."

Kelly carefully turned on the heat under a frying pan and got the hamburgers ready. Then she turned to face Maya. "He was not," she said grumpily. "I thought you looked fantastic! No one else would have criticized you the way he did."

Maya opened the toaster oven and arranged hamburger buns on the grid. "Maybe that's a good thing," she said. "Maybe everyone has been too easy on me so far. Maybe I need someone tougher, to make me as good as I can be."

"I don't know," Kelly said. "Did you really think he was right? I thought you had practically perfect form."

"That's just it," Maya said, starting to slice tomatoes. "*Practically* perfect. Not *perfect.* If I'm going to be a contender at the Olympics one day, I need to get closer to actual perfection."

"Well, he practically destroyed Candace," Kelly said. "She was so bummed afterward I wouldn't be surprised if she skipped class tomorrow."

"Candace was pretty weak," Maya pointed out. "Didn't you think he was on target with the others too? In fact, the only one I thought he was wrong about was you—he was too hard on you. You did a great job—much better than he gave you credit for."

"Still," Kelly admitted, putting the hamburger patties in the pan, "he was right about my not piking as quickly as I should have. If I piked quicker, my feet would be in a better position to nail the landing."

"You already nailed the landing," Maya argued, ripping lettuce into little bits.

"I would nail the landing *better,*" Kelly explained. She poked at a burger with her spatula.

The kitchen door swung open, and Emma and Dimitri came in.

"Hi, girls," Dimitri said. "Everything under control? Should I set the table?"

"Yes, please, Papa," Maya said.

"What is that awful smell?" Emma asked, wrinkling her nose and sniffing the air.

Kelly looked at her. "Um, dinner?"

Frowning, Emma said, "No, really."

"I'm making hamburgers," Kelly reminded her. "I don't smell anything bad."

"Oh, I . . ." Suddenly Emma went pale and turned and pushed through the swinging door to the hall.

"What's the deal?" Kelly demanded, her spatula hanging by her side. "Earlier Mom said she *wanted* hamburgers. Now they smell awful. What's her problem?"

"Maybe she's just tired, Kellinka," Dimitri said. He quickly put down his handful of silverware. "I'll go see." He rushed out after Emma.

Kelly and Maya looked at each other.

"Too weird," Kelly whispered. "If Mom has a stomach bug, why doesn't she just stay in bed? It's like she's sick one minute and fine the next."

"Pass the ketchup, please," Emma said, opening her hamburger bun and sprinkling salt on the patty.

Kelly stared at her from across the table. "Earth to Mom," she said. "One, just half an hour ago you thought these burgers were about as appealing as old sneakers. Two, you *never* use salt."

Emma beamed at her and shrugged. "I can't

help it, sweetie. These burgers taste great. You guys did a wonderful job with dinner. Are there any fries left?"

Wordlessly Maya scooped more French fries onto Emma's plate. Dimitri looked over at his wife and smiled.

"So, girls," he said, changing the subject. "What was your impression of Lugo today?"

Kelly exchanged a quick glance with Maya. "Well, he seems to really know what he's talking about," she said carefully.

"Good, good," Dimitri said. "He has an excellent reputation, you know. And of course, he's famous for having coached many Olympic medalists."

"Yeah, of course," Kelly said.

"Papa, I thought Lugo seemed a little . . . mean with some of the Silvers," Maya put in. "Some of them might have had their feelings hurt."

Like me and Maya, Kelly thought.

"Was Lugo wrong in his criticism?" Dimitri asked with a frown.

Maya shook her head. "No, not exactly. He had some good points. He's just . . . very demanding."

"Mayichka," Dimitri said seriously. "The Silver Stars are just one step below the Gold Stars, who are very, very serious about their gymnastics. It might not be a bad thing for the Silvers to come under a little heat now. It won't be long before you are all competing seriously. Lugo can prepare you for that."

"Yeah, that's what we figured," Maya said, glancing at Kelly.

"Yeah," Kelly agreed slowly. "I guess we just have to get used to his style." She looked at Maya, and Maya shrugged. "Anyway," Kelly said to change the subject, "what's on the Olympics tonight?"

"Um, I think women's track," Emma answered.

"Borrring," Maya said.

Chapter Six

On Wednesday the Silvers didn't rush to Sugarloaf Gymnastic Academy quite as fast as they had the day before, but they still arrived at the gym early.

Maya and the others changed quickly in the locker room. Maya had decided that being coached by Lugo was going to be a good experience. Papa was right—girls not much older than she were already professional gymnasts. She had to be even more serious about gymnastics. That meant paying attention to Lugo and doing exactly what he said. After all, what was more important: competing in the Olympics one day, or her feelings?

"We are so happening," Harry teased, snapping her hair elastic into place. "Look at us—we're early. I don't think I've been early in months."

"It's better this way," Monica said as they walked out of the locker room. "Something tells me this isn't a good week to be late."

As soon as Monica finished speaking, the girls practically ran into Lugo, who was waiting for them by the warm-up barre. He glanced at his watch and frowned.

"Hello, Silvers," he said without a smile. "Where have you been? You're late. It's twenty minutes after three. Why were you not here earlier?"

"Um, actually," Kathryn said, "our class doesn't start till three-thirty. We're a bit early."

"We don't get out of our regular school until three o'clock," Maya explained. "Then we have to get here and change."

Lugo put one hand on his hip and looked almost dumbfounded. "Regular school?" he repeated in his Bulgarian accent. "Why are you still in regular school? Haven't your parents arranged to get tutors for you so you can concentrate on what's important?"

Kelly blinked. "Some of the Golds have tutors, but we Silvers still go to day school. Sometimes we have to miss it if we're competing or have to go to an out-of-town meet, but usually we just go to our regular school and then come here."

"We come here four days a week," Candace reminded him. "Only Golds come six days a week. We're all only eleven or twelve years old."

Lugo waved his hand through the air dismissively. "Winners are formed by the time they're seven or eight years old. Often by the time they're eleven or twelve it's too late. I can see I have much work to do with you girls. Let's not waste time." He looked at his watch. "We will start on the uneven parallel bars. Emma tells me you are learning the hecht. You should have mastered it two years ago, but no matter. Let's go."

"We haven't warmed up yet," Kelly said hesitantly. Both Emma and Dimitri were real sticklers about warming up properly before class. They believed it helped avoid muscle strain and injuries.

A muscle twitched in Lugo's cheek. He really looked irritated.

"I give you ten minutes," he said brusquely, waving them over to the floor mats and glancing at his watch again. Then he turned and walked over to Julie Stiller, who was working with Emma on the vault.

"Geez," Candace muttered. "He's got to lighten up."

"Maybe not," Harry said thoughtfully, beginning to do her stretches. "Maybe he's right—maybe we've had it too easy up till now."

Maya nodded, putting one leg on the barre and

leaning over till her head touched her knee. "This might be the real test," she said. "Lugo might be the thing that separates future Gold Stars from just regular students."

Candace frowned. "I guess I won't be around much longer, then."

Maya met Harry's eyes. Candace had a point. She was getting better at gymnastics all the time, but she *was* the weakest Silver Star. And she'd never had plans to try for the Olympics. She was just taking gymnastics because she enjoyed it. Did that mean that Lugo was going to weed her out?

"All right, girls," Lugo said a few minutes later. "Now you are all warmed up, yes? So let's try the hecht on the uneven bars. Who wants to go first?"

"I'll start," Harry said. "But I'm still working on putting the elements together. Emma has been spotting me. I'll show you what I've done so far."

"No!" Lugo said, clapping his hands. "Do you know how to do the hecht or not?"

"Well, yes," Harry said in surprise. "I know *how*. But I haven't—"

"Then do it." Lugo pointed at the uneven bars. "Now."

Harry glanced at Maya, her surprise showing clearly on her face. Emma and Dimitri never pressured someone to do something if the person didn't feel ready. Harry didn't know if she was ready or not. She had never put all the elements together, though she understood how it was done. Now Lugo wanted her to just jump in.

But he's a very famous coach, she reminded herself. *He must know what he's doing. He must sense that I'm ready, even if I don't know it myself.*

Taking a deep breath, Harry quickly chalked her hands, then jumped up to grab the top bar. Remembering all the advice Emma had given her, she started swinging higher and harder, until her body was bumping the lower bar on the downswing.

Then, when the momentum felt right, she swung hard, let go, and curled around the lower bar. Suddenly she panicked, but there was nothing to hold on to. She had to follow through. Feeling frightened, she let her body circle the lower bar. The momentum took her up and out. Instinctively she stretched her arms overhead and got ready to land feetfirst. Almost before she knew it, her feet slapped against the crash mat. Automatically she assumed the "touchdown" position that every gymnast uses after a landing. Then it dawned on her: She had done it! She had performed a hecht with no help at all!

Smiling but still feeling unsure of herself, she

walked off the mat. Her fellow Silver Stars were cheering and clapping. Harry glanced up at her new coach. Lugo looked satisfied.

"There, you see? You did it. We'll work on technique later. Remember that fear is a useless emotion. It's for babies. You want a big result, you make a big try. Okay, who's next?"

"I'll go," Candace said bravely. "That looked so cool."

Harry wasn't sure that was a good idea. She was still feeling the aftereffects of being scared in the middle of the hecht. If it had almost caused her to make a mistake, how would Candace, who was famous for wanting to plunge ahead before she was ready, react? Emma, Dimitri, and Susan Lu kept Candace reined in as much as possible so that she wouldn't hurt herself. Now Lugo would have to do the same thing.

The coach regarded Candace silently. Then he nodded. "Go ahead," he said.

Harry practically gasped. Candace wasn't ready to try the hecht! Sure, Emma had taken her through the steps. But Candace had a lot more work to do before she tried it solo. Lugo had seen their abilities the day before—he must know she wasn't ready. Harry glanced first at Maya, then at Kelly, and saw they were thinking the same thing.

But Candace trotted happily to the high bar. She chalked her hands and jumped up. Once, twice, three times she swung around. Then she let go and bent sharply at the waist. Momentum carried her around the low bar, her hands out to the sides. But she hadn't gotten quite enough speed and her body uncurled too soon. She dropped heavily to the mats.

From the sidelines Harry saw that Candace had landed hard and unevenly on one ankle. It bent awkwardly beneath her, and Candace yelped.

Instantly Kathryn ran forward to help her twin up. "Are you okay?" she asked.

Frowning, Candace stood and tried to put some weight on her left foot. She grimaced. "Yeah. I guess I just twisted it a little."

"You weren't ready to try the hecht, you dummy," Kathryn said sternly.

"Excuse me, Kathryn," Lugo said, standing in front of the two girls. "That is not your judgment to make. You are still a student, yes? That means you have much to learn. Now, please let go of Candace. She must try the dismount again."

"Again?" Candace repeated in surprise.

Lugo nodded firmly. "You must try again right away so you are not afraid. Go on."

Hesitantly Candace limped back to the bars. Then she turned to look at her teammates. Harry tried to send her a silent message—"Don't do it. You could hurt yourself."

But Lugo was gazing at her impassively, his

arms folded across his chest. Candace slowly rubbed more chalk on her hands.

"Um, maybe Candace should go to the first aid room," Kelly said uncertainly.

Lugo looked at her. "Who are you, her mother?" Not waiting for a reply, he gestured to Candace to begin.

Candace jumped up and began her swings. After four strong swings, Lugo said, "Now!"

Instantly Candace released the top bar and curled around the lower one, keeping her body tight and her knees straight.

"Now!" Lugo said again. Candace immediately straightened her body and sailed up off the lower bar and away from the apparatus. She managed to straighten in time to land, but when her left foot hit the mat she gasped and crumpled to the ground.

Lugo strode over and pulled her to her feet. "There," he said with satisfaction. "You did it. You did not do it well, but you made a start."

"My ankle hurts," Candace said, holding her foot off the ground.

Letting go of her, Lugo shook his head. "Winners don't complain. Winners don't grumble about every splinter in their finger. You did the move—that's what counts. If you can't perform, then quit wasting my time."

He put his hands on his hips, not looking at

Candace again. "Who will go next? Or are you all scared babies? Is this the Silver Star group or the Twinklers?"

Harry's teeth clenched, and she stepped forward to put her arm around Candace, who looked devastated by Lugo's criticism. Harry couldn't believe Candace had done as well as she had the second time.

Candace slowly limped toward the group of Silver Stars.

"Candace?"

Harry was relieved to hear Emma's voice, and she looked up to see her favorite coach heading toward them.

"Candace, are you limping?" Emma asked with concern.

"I landed on my ankle funny," Candace said, not mentioning that she had done the hecht.

"Well, come on," Emma said briskly. "You know better than to walk around on bruised muscles. Let's get you to the first aid room and put ice on it before it gets any worse."

Candace nodded silently, not meeting Lugo's eyes.

After giving Emma a pleasant smile, Lugo ignored them and acted as if Candace didn't exist.

"Who will be next?" he asked with cool sarcasm. "Is there anyone daring enough?"

"I'll go," Kathryn said, an angry flush rising in

her cheeks. Harry knew how she felt. Lugo might be one of the world's best coaches, but he sure didn't know how to be supportive or encouraging.

Then Kathryn did a fabulous hecht off the uneven bars. Anger had made her sharp and precise and determined. Lugo looked almost pleased when she landed straight as a knife, a stiff expression on her face.

Harry sighed. Was Lugo trying to get great work out of them by making them angry and defensive? She hated to admit it, but if that was his plan, it might just be working.

Chapter Seven

"Oh, quick, there's Beau Jarrett!" Kelly whispered on Friday afternoon. Monica was sitting across from Kelly in the back booth at Gianelli's ice cream shop, a few stores down from SGA.

"Where? Where?" Monica cried, her head swiveling like an office chair.

Kelly giggled and took another lick of her cherry-nut-crunch cone.

Monica turned an accusing stare on her. "Very funny," she muttered. "Someday you'll have a crush on someone, and then I'm going to torture *you* about it."

"Don't hold your breath," Kelly advised her. "Gymnastics is my only love."

"Thank heavens we don't have class today," Harry said, sliding into the booth across from Kelly.

"I can't believe you said that," Kelly said, her eyes wide. "You love gymnastics."

"I know," Harry said, taking the wrapper off her straw. "I do love gymnastics. I just don't love Lugo Bigue."

"Me neither," Candace said, sighing as she sat down. "TGIF!"

"How's your ankle?" Harry asked her. "It didn't seem to bother you yesterday, or today at school."

Candace shook her head. "It's ninety-five percent fine," she said. "No biggie."

"It could have been a biggie," Kelly said. She felt angry all over again, thinking about how easily Candace could have been hurt. "General Lu's career screeched to a halt when she hurt herself."

"Yeah," Kathryn said. "So did you learn anything?"

Candace stuck her tongue out at her twin.

"Listen, y'all, quit picking on each other. I want to talk about Lugo," Kelly said.

"We have been talking about Lugo," Maya pointed out. She licked neatly around the edge of her double cone.

"Well, we need to talk about what we're going to do," Kelly continued. "I mean, Lugo is here on a two-week tryout. What if Mom and Dimitri decide to hire him forever?"

"We don't have any say about that," Kathryn said.

"What have Emma and Dimitri said about him?" Monica asked.

Kelly glanced at Maya. "I think they're really glad to have another full-time coach," Kelly said slowly.

"They've been getting home earlier at night, and they haven't had to work so hard," Maya put in.

"They've both been more cheerful lately, and they have more energy," Kelly said.

"The thing about Lugo is, as awful as he is sometimes, well, I sort of feel that he has a couple of things going for him," Harry said.

"You're kidding!" Candace exclaimed. "Like what?"

Harry took a sip of her milk shake. "He's really, really good at the technical stuff," she said. "Sometimes I know I'm doing something just a tiny bit wrong, but I have no idea how to fix it. Lugo always knows. It's almost eerie. He can tell me to unbend just a fraction of a second earlier, and it'll make all the difference. I hate to say it, but I feel like I'm improving because of him."

Kathryn nodded reluctantly. "I know what Harry means. He might be a total slavedriver, but when he's right about something, he's right."

"I don't believe this," Candace said. "You are such a traitor. You heard what he said to me!"

Kathryn nodded again. "He's said mean things

to all of us—and all of the Gold Stars too. I saw him make Taylor Levi cry yesterday because she kept forgetting to point her toes. And he said I looked like the ugly duckling—except I was never going to turn into a swan."

"He told me I might as well take up basketball," Monica said. "Because I'm so tall."

Kelly groaned and put her head in her hands. "He's awful! But he's really good too. That's what makes it so hard. And Maya—tell everyone what Mom said last night."

Maya crunched her cone. "Kelly and I were downstairs last night, working on the beam with Emma, after dinner."

The other Silvers nodded. They all knew that Kelly and Maya had a mini-gym set up in their basement.

"Mom said that both Maya and I looked sharper, crisper," Kelly reported.

"I mean, she noticed a difference in our form after only three classes with Lugo," Maya said.

"Yeah, three whole days of him terrorizing you," Monica said dryly.

"Anyway, that's what's so awful. The last three days have been a real drag," Kelly said. "Lugo has taken every bit of fun out of gymnastics for me. Every bit of fun except the fun of . . . getting better. Getting really good." She shrugged uncomfortably.

"So am I just a wimp, then?" Candace demanded. " 'Cause I totally hate him."

"Me too," Monica said.

"No, you guys aren't wimps," Harry said. "Like it or not, you two are getting better yourselves."

"We are?" Monica said in surprise.

Kelly nodded. "Yeah. You're so worried about him coming down on you that you've been doing everything extra well lately."

"Oh." Monica looked confused.

"Look, let's give him a few more days," Harry said. "Maybe Emma and Dimitri will hire someone else. If we have to put up with him for a few more classes, that's not too bad."

"Yeah," Kelly agreed quietly. "I guess that's not too bad."

Chapter Eight

On Monday after school, Maya walked the eight blocks to SGA by herself.

Kelly and Monica had asked her to go with them to Cochran Park to lie in the sun and listen to the latest Peace Event CD, but Maya had passed on the invitation. She wanted to go to the gym. Back in Russia she had often gone to her father's gym when she didn't have class. It was a chance for her to hang out, watch the Gold Stars, and work on her skills without the pressure of an actual class.

After she pushed open the double glass doors, Maya paused for a moment. The gym almost felt like home now. The sights, sounds, smells—all helped make SGA a place where Maya felt comfortable, happy, and excited. She wasn't going to let Lugo Bigue get in the way of that.

In the locker room she changed into a plain black leotard and braided her hair up. Out in the main room, she saw Dimitri working with the Gold Star boys on the high bar and saw Lugo working with the Gold Star girls on their floor exercises. Susan Lu had the Twinklers, and Emma wasn't around.

Maya warmed up slowly and thoroughly by herself in front of the wall mirrors. She took the time to stretch each muscle and get it loose, ready to move. Since no one was spotting her, she wasn't allowed to work on the uneven bars, but she decided to practice some simple moves on the beam and the vault—whatever equipment wasn't being used by other classes.

When Dimitri saw her he blew her a kiss, and she grinned. Then she stepped up on the two-foot-high practice beam and did some slow, careful walkovers, concentrating on maintaining perfect form.

"Ah! Maya Resnikov!"

Maya stopped to see Lugo smiling at her, his arms crossed over his chest.

"Hi, Lugo," she said.

"You don't have class today, but still you come to the gym and work out," he said. "That's very good. You have initiative, unlike the others. I don't see any of your teammates here."

"They have other stu—" Maya began, feeling defensive about her friends.

"No, no, you have real dedication," Lugo interrupted. "I'm glad to see Dimitri's daughter showing her strength. Today I work with the Golds, but I will spare you a few minutes here and there, all right?"

Maya sighed silently. "All right." What could she say—"No thanks"?

Half an hour later Lugo had her jump some simple vaults, moves she'd been performing since she was five years old.

"Your back is too curved," he told her. "You must go over the vault as if an invisible wall is right behind you, pushing you along and keeping your back very straight."

Maya nodded. She had never thought of it that way before. On her next vault she focused on the image of a wall stuck to her back.

"Very good," Lugo said in his brisk way. "Better."

"That looked excellent, Mayichka," Dimitri said as he passed the vault on his way to his office. "Well done."

Maya smiled happily at her father.

"That was better," Lugo repeated when Dimitri was gone. "It is a fault of yours that you do not carry your shoulders straight enough. You should stand and move and do everything as if you had a clothes hanger in your shirt, keeping your shoulders way back." He pulled on her shoulders. "If you do that, you look much better, like a champion. You move much better. Judges notice you. That is how winners look. Losers look all hunched over, like old women. You do not want to look like an old woman, do you?"

"No," Maya said, inspecting her new posture in the mirror. "Speaking of winners, I used to know Galina Churovna back in Russia, when I was little. I was so happy to see her at the last Olympics."

Lugo snorted and waved his hand dismissively. "Pah! Don't mention her name to me. What a huge disappointment she was. I wasted years on her."

Maya was shocked. "What do you mean? She won a silver medal!"

"Yes, only a silver," Lugo said. "If she had worked harder and kept her mind on her gymnastics, she could have won a gold."

"But she lost the gold by only a few hundredths of a point."

"A few hundredths of a point is like the Grand Canyon!" Lugo snapped. "But no. Galina was weak, a loser. She whined, she complained, she faked injuries. I should have dropped her long before she embarrassed me by winning only a silver."

Maya was so dismayed to hear him speak that way about a gymnast she admired that she didn't know what to say. A moment later Lugo motioned her to the springboard again to try another vault.

"Come, Maya," he said. "Show me a somersault vault. I know *you* will not disappoint me."

Swallowing, Maya went down to the runway to gain momentum. Lugo might not realize it, but he had such impossible expectations for people that *everyone* was going to disappoint him sooner or later. Even her.

"Miss Candace!" Lugo snapped on Tuesday afternoon. "What is the joke? You have something to say to the class?"

Candace jumped and flushed with embarrassment. Kelly sighed to herself. She had seen Candace lean over to whisper something to Harry, and right then Kelly had known what was coming. Lugo hated it when anyone looked as if she wasn't paying attention. It was only four-thirty, but it felt as if they had been in class about ten hours.

So far Lugo had criticized Harry for looking a tiny bit scared when she performed her hecht again. It didn't matter that she had done a fabulous job. Fear was for babies, losers. Judges hated to see fear. Then he had pretended that Monica's leopard-print leotard was giving him a headache.

From then on, he said, everyone had to come to class looking more professional, less flashy. Monica had bit her lip and brushed a hand quickly across her eyes. Kelly wanted to comfort her but didn't dare. It would have to wait until after class.

"Well?" Lugo barked now, his arms crossed over his chest.

"No," Candace mumbled, looking at the floor.

"I didn't think so," Lugo said scathingly. He turned his attention back to Kathryn, who was working on a salto-with-a-half-twist dismount from the balance beam.

"Now, your feet are too close together," he said firmly. "Keep them five inches apart—no more, no less. Like this. It will make you more stable and help you land properly."

"Oh, I see," Kathryn said, nodding. She took a few running steps on the beam and launched into the dismount again. This time she held her landing better.

Kelly kept her face blank. In the old days—B.L., Before Lugo—they all would have cheered and clapped. But Lugo said cheering and clapping were for amateurs. If Kathryn came in first in an important competition, they would be allowed to cheer and clap. Not before.

"Good," Lugo said briskly. "Better. You will try that five more times before next class, yes?"

"Yes," Kathryn said.

"Now, Kelly." Lugo gestured to the beam.

Kelly had practiced a salto with a half twist before, on the floor mats. It was an important basic move that really jazzed up routines in the floor exercise, the beam, and the vault. In another six months they would all be working on saltos with a full twist, and then saltos with a twist and a half, and then saltos with a double twist . . .

Kelly mounted the beam and focused her thoughts. She would need momentum. She needed to bounce high, tucking quickly and letting her speed carry her through. Her toes had to be pointed, her arms tucked at her sides, her eyes straight ahead. She took a deep breath and began.

Quickly she ran a few steps down the beam, already seeing herself performing the move in her mind. She launched into the salto, concentrating on keeping perfect form, and turned in the air, head over heels and to the side at the same time. A split second later she uncoiled and shot her feet out to make the landing. The floor rushed up a fraction of a second before she expected it, and her left foot landed hard against the thick mat. She held the landing but couldn't help wincing as she felt her ankle protest.

When she realized she had nailed the move, Kelly threw her arms overhead and grinned triumphantly.

Lugo motioned her back to the side. "Your form was acceptable," he said, "but I do not want to see any wincing. What will judges think if they see you wincing? They will deduct points. You will lose to someone who did not wince. Toughen up."

Two bright red spots burned in Kelly's cheeks. She had done a good job, she had nailed the landing, and still Lugo criticized her. *Next time,* she vowed to herself, *I'll keep my face blank even if I break a bone.*

"Now, Maya," Lugo said, pointing at the beam. "Go."

Kelly knew her stepsister well enough to know that Maya was feeling a fierce determination to do well. Her eyes were focused forward, her jaw set in a hard line. She walked stiffly to the beam and climbed up without looking at anyone. Her face was like a mask.

Moving with precise, perfect movements, Maya took several running steps and threw herself into a salto with a half twist. Kelly drew in a breath. She didn't see any flaws at all in Maya's form. Her stepsister landed like a ramrod, bending her knees to absorb the impact but sticking the landing.

Kelly glanced quickly at Monica, standing next to her. Monica nodded. Maya had done it perfectly.

Kelly waited, her arms crossed over her chest.

Let Lugo try to criticize Maya! Her move had been absolutely textbook perfect. No one could have done better. Feeling proud of Maya, Kelly grinned and nodded at her as she walked breathlessly off the mats.

Maya's eyes held a tiny satisfied glint. She knew she had done well.

"Good form," Lugo said, sounding almost grudging. "But you have no sparkle, no personality. Judges like to see sparkle. It's no use looking like a robot."

Kelly's jaw almost dropped with outrage. Even perfection wasn't good enough! She looked at Maya to see her reaction. Maya was stone-faced, but she merely nodded. Kelly couldn't believe her stepsister's self-control.

"I'll sparkle him," Monica said under her breath.

"Silver Stars, gather around," Lugo said, motioning them closer. "I have an announcement. Part of my responsibility as a coach is to prepare you for competitions, yes? So, in order to get you used to a more realistic system of judging, I'm setting up a demerit schedule."

Kelly could feel her eyes about to pop out of her head, but she didn't trust herself to speak.

"Small infractions earn one demerit," he continued. "Larger mistakes earn more. Infractions include speaking during class, not being prepared for class, wearing inappropriate clothing, and so on. Once you have five demerits, you will run around the gym twenty times, as well as write a two-page paper on why you want to sabotage your gymnastics career. Ten demerits and you're out of the Silver Stars. This will go into effect tomorrow. Up till now, I've been going easy on you. But you are all far behind in your training. It's time to separate the winners from the losers."

Taking out a pen, he wrote something down on his clipboard while the Silvers stared at him in shocked silence.

Finally Candace couldn't stand it anymore. Kelly motioned to her to keep quiet, but the red-haired girl ignored her.

"You're kidding," Candace said. "Right?"

Without even looking up, Lugo said, "That's one demerit for you. Keep it up, Miss Candace." He wrote something down on his clipboard.

I don't believe this. Gymnastics has become a bad dream, Kelly thought. It would be only a matter of days before Candace was kicked off the team. And how long would it take for the others? How long would it take before there were no Silver Stars at all?

Chapter Nine

"Be careful with that straw wrapper, Miss Harry," Candace said dryly at lunch on Wednesday. "I don't want to have to give you a demerit."

Harry groaned and crumpled her wrapper as Maya slid into a chair. Lunch was the only time during the school day when all the Silver Stars could get together and talk. Since Kathryn, Candace, and Harry were in sixth grade, they didn't have any classes with Monica, Maya, and Kelly, who were in seventh.

There was a table in the middle of the last row by the windows where they usually met. The cafeteria was noisy, filled with talking students. Maya liked the cafeteria with its smells of cooking food, and the sunlight flooding the windows, and the view of the playground outside. She liked being surrounded by the students of the middle school. She was glad that her father had decided to let her go to regular school, just as Kelly and the other Silvers did.

Maya opened her insulated lunch bag and pulled out a sandwich, a banana, and three cookies. She smiled. Kelly had made a good lunch today. They took turns making both their lunches so they had to do it only every other day.

"Who watched the divers last night?" Monica asked.

"I did," said Harry. "Patti Belleport was so graceful."

"Monica, who are you trying to kid?" Candace said. "You know you just like seeing the guys in their Speedos."

Everyone laughed, and Monica blushed.

"That's not true!" she protested.

Kelly came to Monica's rescue. She pointed a finger at Candace. "Miss Candace, no jokes," she said gruffly. "One demerit."

"This whole demerit thing is totally crazy," Monica said, grateful for the change in subject.

"I've heard of other coaches who use demerits," Maya said tentatively. "It's not unusual."

Candace turned wide green eyes on her teammate. "Maya! You can't be sticking up for him!"

"No, no," Maya said quickly. "I'm just saying that there *are* other coaches who use demerits sometimes."

"Emma and Dimitri don't use demerits," Kathryn said, sliding her tray onto the table and sitting down.

"Yeah," Monica said, eating a spoonful of yogurt. "I thought I was nervous before, but now I feel like I'm getting ulcers."

"I think we should tell Emma and Dimitri," Harry said. She opened her milk and put her straw in.

Maya met Kelly's eyes across the table.

"Well, you know," Kelly said slowly, "Lugo's only going to be here for a few more days. His two weeks will be up Saturday." She had done some thinking and had decided that Lugo couldn't be that much of a threat. Not if he was leaving so soon.

"Yeah," Maya said. "And really, who could run up ten demerits before then?"

"Me," Candace said immediately, taking a bite of cookie.

"Me," Monica added.

Maya snapped a carrot stick in two. "Even if you could run up ten demerits," she said, "and Lugo kicked you off the team, all we have to do is go to Emma and Papa after Lugo leaves and explain the reason to them. As long as you're following the gym rules, I'm sure they would keep you on the Silvers."

"Maya's right," Kelly said. "Lugo doesn't run everything. Can you guys just try to keep it together until he leaves after Saturday?"

"I guess," Monica said doubtfully. "But why don't you want us to tell Emma and Dimitri? Is it because Lugo isn't hassling you guys as much as he's hassling the rest of us?"

"Monica!" Kelly said. "You know that's not true. Remember what he told me about wincing yesterday?"

"And he said I had no sparkle." Maya frowned. "No one can please him."

"Maya and I already told you that we don't want to say anything to Mom and Dimitri because they seem a lot happier," Kelly said. "I mean, Mom's been feeling sick, off and on, but in general they're doing better since they have a full-time coach at SGA. Mom even made dinner last night."

"Well, okay," Kathryn said. "I guess they do deserve a break. But just tell me one thing: What are we going to do if your parents want to hire Lugo permanently?"

Maya sighed and rested her head in her hands. "I don't know," she admitted.

"We haven't thought that far ahead," Kelly said. "Let's just keep our fingers crossed that it doesn't happen."

"Okay," Kathryn said.

The Silvers ate their lunches silently.

"Question," Maya said a few minutes later.

"What?" Kelly asked.

"Why are my fingers crossed, and how long do I have to keep them that way?" She held up the hand holding her sandwich. Her fingers were still crossed. When the other Silver Stars burst out laughing, she looked mystified.

"Hi, Monica," Susan Lu said as Monica started warming up in front of the mirrors. "You're the first one here."

"You're kidding," Monica said, a pleased smile on her face. "I'm never first." She leaned over and began stretching her leg muscles.

Kelly trotted up and assumed a position beside Monica. "Gosh, I almost didn't recognize you," she said jokingly.

Monica scowled. It had taken her half an hour to find the plain gray leotard at the bottom of her closet. It was the least flashy one she owned. Her brown curls were gathered into a simple knot, held in place with a hair elastic. That was it. Monica felt about as attractive as a storm cloud.

"How is Beau going to notice me if I look like this?" Monica whispered as she and Kelly swept their arms overhead in a full-body stretch. "And what difference does it make what I wear, anyway?"

"It matters if you don't want to get a demerit, Miss Monica," Kelly said in a gruff voice, trying to imitate Lugo's accent.

Monica giggled as Harry, Kathryn, and Maya walked up. Candace was a minute behind them.

"Hi, girls," Susan said, marking off their attendance on her clipboard. "Emma went for a checkup today at the doctor's, so Lugo is working with the Gold Stars, and I'm working with you."

"Really?" Monica said, feeling a smile spreading over her face. "Fabulous!"

Susan looked surprised. "I'm glad you think so," she said with a smile of her own. "I'm going to go arrange the mats by the balance beam. We're going to work on your saltos with a half twist today. Be sure to warm up each muscle group thoroughly."

"All right!" Candace cheered, punching the air. Again Susan gave her a surprised and pleased look.

Once the teacher was gone, Monica hurried through the rest of her warm-up. "You know, we used to call her General Lu because she seemed so strict. But compared to Lugo, she's a walk in the park."

"Who's walking in the park?" Maya asked.

"She means Susan's nice and easy compared to

Lugo," Monica explained. Though Maya spoke English almost perfectly, she still didn't understand some expressions. Or some superstitions, like crossing your fingers.

"Oh," Maya said, nodding. "Compared to Lugo, *anyone's* going for a walk in the park."

"Uh, yeah, right," Kelly said, smiling. "Sort of."

Now this is more like it, Monica thought half an hour later. It was just like old times B.L.—Before Lugo. Her teammates were relaxed, smiling and joking. And that didn't mean they were any less serious about gymnastics—just that they were enjoying training again.

"Okay, now make sure those toes are pointed on the twist, and keep your knees tightly together. If your form is sloppy, you'll spin out of control," Susan instructed Harry.

"Okay," Harry said happily. Her eyes focused in concentration as she collected herself on the beam. Then she took several running steps and launched herself into a perfect salto with a half twist. Sailing off the beam, she snapped her feet down to nail the landing. Triumphantly she threw her arms overhead.

"Excellent, Harry!" Susan exclaimed, a wide smile on her face. "Terrific job."

Harry beamed, then walked to the side.

Monica raised her hand for a high five. "Way to go."

"It's easier when I don't have to worry about Lugo," Harry whispered.

"No, no! You idiot!"

Monica jumped at the sound of the harsh voice across the gym. She and the other Silver Stars turned curiously to see Lugo yelling at . . . Beau Jarrett.

Monica gasped and covered her mouth with her hand. Beau was angry, his face flushed. He was looking at the floor, his hands clenched into fists by his sides.

"How many times I tell you!" Lugo yelled, standing over him. "You keep your arms straight when you do a crossover on the high bar. Uneven, you look sloppy, like a loser. I told you twice! How did you get to be a Gold Star? You should be a Twinkler! You should sit with the babies!"

Beau looked up and glared at the coach. The other Gold Stars looked surprised and cowed by Lugo's anger.

Monica could tell that Beau was humiliated and angry, and she didn't blame him. Lugo was a jerk! Where was Dimitri when Lugo was yelling at SGA's most promising male Gold Star? She looked around but didn't see Dimitri. He must be in the office, she figured, or maybe he had taken Emma to the doctor.

"Do it again." Lugo motioned to the high bar.

"Girls," Susan said gently to get their attention. "I need you to concentrate on this move. Now, who's next for the salto? Maya?"

"Yes." Maya stepped onto the beam. Monica could see her trying to gather her thoughts. All the Silvers were visibly shaken by what they had seen Lugo do. But Susan didn't seem to have any reaction—she wasn't even looking at Lugo.

Monica glanced back to see Beau doing giant swings on the high bar. Only male gymnasts performed on the high bar. It was like the uneven parallel bars, minus the lower bar.

"Monica."

Monica turned back to face Susan Lu.

"Please keep your mind on your own class," the assistant coach said gently. "When your mind wanders, you're in more danger of making a mistake. That's when you're at risk of injuring yourself."

"Yes, ma'am," Monica said.

Maya did her salto with a half twist almost perfectly, but she wobbled on the landing and had to wave her arms to keep her balance.

"Good effort, Maya," Susan said with a smile. "Next time tuck your knees in a bit tighter and pull out of the spin a fraction sooner. Then you'll be in a better position to land."

"I see. Okay," Maya said.

"Better," Monica heard Lugo bark across the gym. "That was better. When you are good, you are very good."

Monica was dying to turn around to see Beau's reaction but didn't dare. Her heart went out to Beau, poor, dear Beau, who was being treated so badly by that monster, Lugo . . .

"Ah, girls," said Dimitri's voice. "How is your lesson?"

"Fine," Harry said.

"Fine," Kelly echoed.

"Good," Dimitri said cheerfully. "Now I'm going to ask Lugo to come work with you. Susan, will you please help the Gold Stars with some dance movements on the floor mats?"

"Will do," Susan said.

It took all Monica's self-control not to groan out loud. *Back with Lugo! What a drag. And after class was going so well, too.*

"Miss Kathryn, do not arch your back so much," Lugo said. Lugo had joined them, and they had sadly watched Susan cross the gym to the Gold Stars. Lugo was taking them through their saltos with a half twist on the balance beam.

"Oh, sorry," Kathryn muttered. She straightened her back.

"Now, I want to see some quick, precise sashays down the beam," Lugo instructed. "Then a tuck jump and a turn. Then the salto, off the end."

"Got it," Kathryn said, frowning in concentration.

Monica and the other Silvers were watching Kathryn from the sidelines. Feeling something warm and fuzzy brush against her bare legs, Monica looked down and saw Sam Gordon Andrew. He dropped a small dead lizard at her feet, then twined around her ankles proudly.

"Oh, lovely," Monica muttered. She forced a smile and whispered, "Good cat. Good boy. What a nice lizard."

Sam Gordon Andrew purred happily and stalked away, his tail in the air.

"Excuse me, Lugo?" Monica said softly. "Can I take a minute to get rid of this thing?"

Lugo looked down at her, and she pointed to the dead lizard on the floor. Lugo nodded once, then looked back at Kathryn.

Monica quickly went to the girls' rest room and got a handful of paper towels. Grimacing, she scooped up the lizard and put it in the trash. When she looked up, she saw Kelly grinning at her, hiding a laugh behind her hand. Monica made a face.

"Miss Monica," Lugo said calmly, "that will be two demerits."

Monica's jaw dropped. "What? Why?"

"You should not have interrupted me to play with the cat," he said, marking her demerits down on his clipboard.

"I wasn't *playing*," Monica said hotly. "Next time I'll leave the stupid lizard there! Besides, you gave me permission!"

Lugo's cold blue eyes looked at her. "One more demerit."

"But she did ask permission," Kelly said angrily. "And you gave it. We all heard you."

"One demerit for Kelly," Lugo said, marking it down. He looked at the other Silver Stars, as if daring them to question him. No one said anything, though Monica could see Harry clenching her teeth, and Candace's eyes were snapping.

Feeling angrier than she ever had in her whole life, Monica crossed her arms and stood silently through the rest of the class. Lugo kept them all ten minutes past their usual quitting time, but no one said a word.

Chapter Ten

"*In*credible," Monica said wearily late that same afternoon.

"That's one word for it," Candace grumbled.

Kelly sighed. Lugo had finally dismissed them. Now she and her teammates were walking to the bus stop one block away from SGA. Since Kelly, Maya, and Monica lived nearby, they usually walked home after gymnastics. But the bus stop was in their direction, and they were keeping Harry, Candace, and Kathryn company.

"Just two more classes, guys," Kelly reminded them. "Thursday and Saturday. Then Lugo's gone for good."

"Maybe I'll be sick tomorrow," Candace said. "I think I feel myself coming down with something."

"Me too," Harry said. "Lugo-itis."

Kelly giggled. "You guys! You can't call in sick. Please don't."

"Yeah," Monica said. "You wouldn't desert the rest of us in our time of need, would you?"

"Yes, I would," Candace said firmly.

"Now, come on," Kelly began, but she was interrupted by the sound of voices behind her.

"Oh, I know," Julie Stiller said. "It's going to be fabulous. He is just absolutely the best."

"You said it," Taylor Levi agreed. "He's tough, but he's good."

Kelly rolled her eyes at Monica. Julie Stiller was such a pain. Kelly pulled Maya closer to her so that the older girls could pass them on the sidewalk.

"Hey, it's the little Silver Stars," Julie said with artificial friendliness.

Kelly looked at her stonily.

"Have you heard the great news?" Taylor said, then laughed behind her hand.

"What news?" Kathryn asked.

"Dimitri and Emma have asked Lugo to stay on another week," Julie said excitedly. "Isn't that great?"

Kelly felt her eyes widen. Beside her, Monica stiffened.

"You're kidding!" Candace cried. "They didn't announce it to our class."

"Nope," Julie said brightly. "Dimitri just told us

Golds about it. I guess he'll tell you youngsters tomorrow."

"Another whole week?" Monica wailed. "It can't be true!"

"Yep." Julie looked smug. "And we Gold Stars are sure that they're trying to iron out a contract for him to stay on permanently. Wouldn't that be fabulous?"

"You have two seconds to tell me you're kidding," Monica said, her eyes narrowed to slits.

"Monica," Julie said in surprise, "don't tell me you're not totally excited about Lugo staying. I mean, he's an incredible coach."

"Incredibly obnoxious, maybe," Candace muttered.

"Hmmm." Julie looked thoughtful. "Well, kids, you know what they say: If you can't stand the heat, get out of the kitchen. Maybe you guys just aren't ready for the big league. Know what I'm saying?"

Not waiting for an answer, Julie and Taylor practically skipped the rest of the way to the bus stop. The Silver Stars stood there gaping.

"That does it," Kathryn muttered sourly. "I'm waiting for the bus after this one."

"What a witch," Monica fumed.

"She *can't* like him," Harry said. "I refuse to believe that she likes him."

"Well, they're both awful people," Kelly pointed out. "Maybe they're drawn to each other somehow."

"You guys are missing the whole point!" Candace cried. "The point is that Lugo is staying for a whole other week—and maybe for good. Don't you see what this means?"

"What?" Maya asked. "That our lives will be miserable for the next ten years or so, until we get out of gymnastics?"

"Or that we'll quit gymnastics?" Monica asked.

"No," Harry said slowly, looking at the ground. "I'm sorry, Kelly and Maya. I know you guys have to stay here. But I'll tell you, I don't want to be miserable for the next ten years, and I don't want to quit gymnastics. I might . . . I might have to leave SGA—and find another gym."

Kelly drew in a quick breath. She looked over at Maya, whose eyes were wide.

"I want to keep working with Emma and Dimitri too," Kathryn said. "But I agree with Harry. I don't want to be miserable. I love gymnastics, but I know I won't love it if I have to work with Lugo. And when I'm a Gold Star, I'd have to work with him six days a week."

"But, Kathryn," Kelly began.

Kathryn held up her hand. "I believe he gets results with his gymnasts," she continued. "I even think I'm better at some things since he started coaching us. We probably all are. But after one of his classes, I always feel terrible, like a loser. I don't want to feel that way all the time. I don't want to hate myself." She kicked at a bottle cap on the ground.

Kelly whirled to face her best friend. "Monica?" she said pleadingly.

Monica sighed and brushed a puffy strand of hair off her forehead. "Kelly, you know I love gymnastics. But if Lugo stays for good, I might go work at Fur, Feather, and Scale all the time. It just wouldn't be worth it to me to put up with his meanness."

Once again Kelly met Maya's eyes. "This does it," Kelly said. "Tonight we have to talk to Mom and Dimitri. Lugo has to be stopped—before the Silver Stars are ruined forever."

Kelly and Maya plodded up the front steps of their big Victorian house. Usually coming home made Kelly feel happy. She loved this house, and she loved the feeling of having a real family—made up of her, Emma, Maya, and Dimitri. It had felt very strange at first, but now she depended on it.

The house seemed quiet and empty when the girls walked in.

Kelly dropped her backpack on the bench in the front hall and glanced at her watch. "Guess they're not back yet. What are we supposed to do about dinner?"

"Um, I think there're some fish sticks in the freezer," Maya said. "We could have them with French fries."

Kelly laughed. "That sounds like a healthy, low-fat meal."

"It's quick and easy," Maya said. "No one said it was healthy."

The swinging door of the kitchen opened, and Dimitri came out, wiping his hands on a kitchen towel. "Ah, girls," he said. "I beat you home, eh?"

"You had a car," Maya pointed out.

"Is Mom here?" Kelly asked. "How did the doctor go?"

"Her checkup was fine," Dimitri said. "He said everything is wonderful, but that your mother needs to get more rest. She's taking a nap right now."

"A nap?" Kelly was amazed. "I don't think Mom has ever taken a nap in her life. Are you sure she's okay?"

Dimitri laughed. "Positive. She's perfect. A nap is no big deal."

The girls followed him back into the kitchen, where Dimitri began to set the table for dinner.

"We were just talking about what to make," Maya told him.

"No need," Dimitri said. "I ordered take-out. The sushi should be arriving any minute."

"Sushi! Mom hates sushi," Kelly said.

Dimitri shrugged. "She had a craving for it. I also got some chicken teriyaki for you, in case you don't want the fish."

"Thanks," Kelly said, pouring herself a glass of juice.

"Ahem." Maya cleared her throat and shot a glance at Kelly. Kelly nodded at her.

"Papa, about Lugo," Maya began. "Is it really true that he's staying another week?"

"Yes," Dimitri said, putting a folded napkin at each place. "Emma and I were very pleased that he could stay. We believe that everyone—including us—will benefit from another week of Lugo's instruction."

Groaning to herself, Kelly put down her glass of juice. Another whole week of torture! And worse, when the rest of the Silvers found out about it, there was going to be mutiny!

"It will give Lugo time to get used to doing things the SGA way," Dimitri continued. He took four plates from a cupboard.

"Instead of the Nazi way," Kelly muttered. Dimitri didn't seem to notice.

"It's so great for Emma and me to have this extra help right now," Dimitri said, turning to smile at Kelly. "In a few weeks everything will be better, and then we can decide what to do. But right now he's making a valuable contribution."

The doorbell rang.

"That must be the sushi now," Dimitri said, going to answer it. "Kelly, could you go wake your mother, please?"

"Okay," Kelly said. She and Maya looked at each other in despair.

"What are we going to do?" Maya whispered. "We'll end up being the only two Silver Stars."

"I know," Kelly said in frustration. "But how can we ask them to get rid of Lugo when he's helping them so much?"

"Yeah," Maya said despondently. "I guess we just have to hang in there until someone comes up with an answer."

"I just hope we don't lose all our friends because of him," Kelly muttered.

Chapter Eleven

On Thursday afternoon Kelly quickly scrambled into her leotard—a plain navy blue one with long sleeves. The Silver Stars were lined up in the locker room, each in front of her locker.

Next to her, Monica threw her school clothes into her duffel. She was wearing a plain, long-sleeved white leotard.

"I look so boring," she complained.

"You look fine," Kelly told her. "You always look fine."

Kathryn was clipping her hair back with bobby pins, holding the extras in her mouth. "Id oo alk oo Imitri?" she mumbled.

Kelly nodded sadly. "It's true. Lugo's staying another week."

"Papa didn't say whether they were asking him to stay forever," Maya said, trying to sound hopeful.

Hannah Goldberg and Sherry Jenkins burst into the locker room, laughing and trying to punch each other. They were both Bronze Stars—Hannah was nine and Sherry was ten.

"Cut it out!" Hannah giggled. "We have to change fast. Today Susan's going to start us on aerial somis on the floor mats."

"You started it!" Sherry pulled open her locker and dumped her duffel bag on the bench. "Aerial somis are going to be so cool! I can't wait."

Kelly looked at the younger girls and sighed. Just a few weeks ago the Silver Stars had been that happy and excited about class. Now they were six glum, unenthusiastic gymnasts.

"I'm just dreading the next week," Harry said quietly. "On the one hand, I think I'm getting better at gymnastics. On the other hand, I have to go through so much stress to get there. And what if Emma and Dimitri ask him to stay permanently? Last night I couldn't sleep because I kept thinking about it."

"Maybe you just don't have what it takes," Julie Stiller said, popping her head over the bank of lockers.

Kelly rolled her eyes. Killer Stiller must have been there the whole time, listening to them!

"Shut up, Julie," Monica said in a steely voice.

"I mean, think about it," Julie went on. "Do you think Olga and Nadia and Dominique and the other Dominique sit around and whine about how tough their coaches are? No. I bet their coaches were ten times as tough as Lugo is. But they wanted to be the best, so they just sucked it up. That's what the Golds are doing. I guess you guys want to sit around and do your nails and chat all the time." Julie closed her locker with a snap. "Well, when I get the gold medal at the Olympics, I'll be sure to wave at you in the stands."

"Look, Julie," Kelly said angrily, "I'm just as serious and dedicated to gymnastics as you are. But I don't think you have to be miserable all the time to get ahead. I know I can be a winner without feeling like I want to cry before every class."

Julie sneered. "You're naive," she said snidely, and flounced out of the locker room.

Kelly looked at Monica, then tossed her hairbrush onto the bench in disgust. "The next time Sam Gordon Andrew has a dead mouse, could you make sure he puts it in *her* locker?"

Monica laughed. "I'll try."

"Girls, girls!" Ten minutes later Lugo stood over the Silver Stars and clapped his hands twice.

Kelly paused in her stretching and glanced up at him. He looked irritated and impatient.

"Come now, you've warmed up enough!" he

said. "Why are you wasting time this way? You baby yourselves with these long warm-ups."

"Emma always says warming up properly is really important," Kathryn said firmly. She took her foot down from the barre and did a handstand.

"I would not go against what Emma says," Lugo replied. "But you have to be more professional, get with the program. In another year or two you will be Gold Stars, and possibly competing internationally. No more slacking off. Now, everyone to the uneven bars."

"Again, Harry," Lugo said. "And this time, try to get more height on your dismount."

"You want me to do the hecht again?" Harry asked, wiping the sweat off her forehead with a towel. "I've already done it four times."

Kelly thought Harry's arms trembled as she draped the towel around the back of her neck.

"You have not done it perfectly yet," Lugo said impassively. "Do it once more. Do you think the judges will excuse you if you are tired?"

"Judges, judges, judges," Candace muttered, risking a demerit. "I'm sick of hearing about the judges this, the judges that."

Silently Kelly agreed with her.

Once more Harry jumped up and hung from

the top bar. Again she started swinging, getting enough momentum to perform the release maneuver. Kelly watched as her friend bit her lip in concentration. Each time Harry had done the move, Lugo had found fault. He wasn't making things up, Kelly admitted. There were some tiny, tiny adjustments that Harry had to make. But she had only learned the dismount two weeks before! Of course she wasn't perfect yet.

"He's being too hard on her," Monica whispered to Kelly from the side of her mouth.

"That's just what I was thinking," Kelly whispered back.

Harry released the top bar, whipped her body around the lower bar, then flew into the air, tucking her arms at her sides. Her toes were pointed, her body perfectly straight. She landed on the crash mats almost eight feet away, and she stuck the landing.

"All right!" Kelly couldn't help yelling. She punched the air, the way she used to when one of her friends did well—B.L.

"Enough, Miss Kelly," Lugo said dryly. "You are not a cheerleader." He turned to Harry, who was wiping her forehead again. "Better," he told her. She almost sagged in relief. "Now, Miss Maya? It is your turn for the hecht."

Kelly watched proudly as her stepsister jumped

up to the top bar. Maya didn't have much practice with the hecht—none of them did—but she was a truly gifted gymnast. Kelly knew she would do the Silvers proud.

But with Maya, too, Lugo found fault.

"Your back was too arched," he told her the first time she performed the dismount. "And you were crooked when you came off for the landing. Make sure your arms are even and tucked at your sides, so you don't go off to one side. Do it again."

The second time, Maya had a bit too much speed coming off the lower bar, so she sailed over the crash mats too far but not high enough. Her landing was sort of a skid on her knees. Kelly put her hand over her eyes for a second. Maya was usually great, but every gymnast made a mistake sometimes. Maya seemed a little rattled.

"Very nice," Lugo said. "Very graceful. Like a swan. A swan with major clumsiness problems. Do it again."

Maya gritted her teeth and jumped up to the high bar again.

This time she did the move almost perfectly. However, right after the release move from the upper to the lower bar, before her body curled around, she clipped her left hand on the bar. Kelly could see her wince. But she released smoothly and made a very good landing.

"That was barely acceptable," Lugo said, crossing his arms on his chest.

Maya was cradling her hand. "I think I bruised my hand," she said tentatively.

Without responding, Lugo took out his clipboard. "One demerit," he said calmly, writing it down. "Judges are not interested in bruises, and neither am I. Your job is to perform. Now do it again."

For a moment Maya stared at him, and so did the other Silver Stars. Was Lugo going to ignore Maya's injury? Kelly couldn't believe that Maya had gotten a demerit for even mentioning it.

"Is there a problem?" Lugo asked, raising his voice.

Maya didn't respond. She looked confused and upset, and Kelly felt herself getting angry on her stepsister's behalf.

"Well?" Lugo practically shouted. "If you can't do it, maybe you should be excused. You can go home and knit. Maybe you do not belong here."

Amazed, Kelly saw Maya's lip tremble. In the four months that Kelly had known her, she had discovered that Maya was very, very tough. Her rigorous early years of training had made her very focused and professional. For Lugo to be getting to her this way was incredible.

Kelly started to step forward, ready to leave with Maya if she decided to go. But Maya took a deep breath, quickly wiped her good hand across her eyes, and went to jump up to the top bar again.

This time it was like watching a textbook demonstration of a hecht. Maya swung exactly the right way, the right number of times, at the right speed. She released perfectly, curled around the lower bar perfectly, then sailed up and out. She really did look like a swan, Kelly thought. Her landing couldn't have been any better.

"That's more like it," Lugo said, letting the ghost of a smile cross his lips. He patted Maya on the shoulder. "See? You think I'm so tough. But you need toughness in order to be the best. Second best is not good enough. Not for Lugo. Not for Maya, either, right?"

Maya shrugged, holding her hurt hand against her chest.

Smiling broadly, Lugo clapped his hands twice. "Take a water break. Back here in two minutes."

As the Silvers headed toward the water fountain, Kathryn murmured, "He's like Jekyll and Hyde."

Kelly agreed. *How can he be so horrible and then be so cheerful?* "Are you okay?" she whispered to Maya.

"Uh-huh." Maya nodded. "But I think I did hurt my hand." She sounded sad.

"This does it," Kelly whispered to her friends as the Silvers gathered around the fountain. "I'm calling an emergency Silvers meeting today at Gianelli's."

Chapter Twelve

"Okay, what are our options?" Kelly said bluntly once her teammates had gotten their ice cream and sat down in their usual booth at Gianelli's.

"That's the problem," Candace said glumly. "Really, the only option we have is to quit."

Maya stirred her milk shake with her good hand. After class she had stopped by the first aid room and gotten some ice, which she was still holding against her wrist. "I can't quit," she said sadly. "Even though he makes me feel about an inch tall."

"If he was leaving after Saturday, it would be no problem," Harry said. "But he'll be here another whole week."

"And maybe a lot longer than that," Kathryn reminded them.

"Look, let's just go to Emma and Dimitri and tell them how we feel," Candace said.

"Yeah, and look like total babies in front of everyone," Monica said.

"I have to agree with Monica," Kelly said reluctantly. "I keep thinking about it and thinking about it, but I can't come up with a solution. I mean, I hate Lugo too, but you know what? None of the Gold Stars have complained about him." What Julie had said in the locker room still rankled her.

"Beau hates him," Monica said. "He treats Beau like dirt—first telling him how awful he is and then saying he's the best Gold Star."

"Oh, well, that decides it," Harry teased her. "If Beau hates him, Lugo has to go."

Monica giggled, looking embarrassed.

"But seriously," Maya said. "I don't want us to look like we can't slice the ketchup."

Kelly looked at her. "Slice the ketchup?" Her brow wrinkled. "Oh. It's *cut the mustard,*" she corrected Maya.

Maya waved her good hand. "Whatever. You know what I mean. If the Gold Stars can hang in there, I hate for us to look as if we can't."

"It's awful, but I keep wondering," Harry said slowly, "what if he's right? Sometimes I wonder if I *am* a total loser and just never knew it before. I used to think I was good at gymnastics."

"You *are* good!" Kelly said. "You're *really* good. Don't let him get to you. Mom always says a gymnast's first tool is a good mental attitude."

"We just have to figure out how to fight him without involving Emma or Papa," Maya said, slurping up the last of her milk shake.

"If only he weren't helping them so much," Kelly said.

"And they really need the help right now. They've been working so hard," Maya agreed.

"Let's be really mean to him," Candace suggested brightly.

"He wouldn't care," Harry said dryly. "He probably wouldn't even notice."

Monica groaned. "I have the feeling we're all going to be running laps and writing essays soon."

"Wait, wait," Kelly said, waving her hands, her eyes shining with excitement. "Oh my gosh, y'all. I just got a brilliant, awful idea."

Chapter Thirteen

I sure hope this plan doesn't backfire, Monica thought as she pushed open the double glass doors at SGA on Saturday morning. *It could blow up right in our faces.*

"Hi," Kelly said with a grin when Monica entered the girls' locker room and tossed her duffel onto a pink bench. "Ready for action?"

Monica sighed. "Ready as I'll ever be."

Jumping up, Kelly checked her hair in the mirror, then tugged down on her leotard. "It's showtime, folks. Everyone remember what to do." With a determined look, she headed out into the gym. Kathryn, Candace, and Maya were right behind her.

Harry was still brushing her hair into a ponytail. "I'm not so sure we should do this," she said.

"Me neither," Monica admitted. "In a way, I'm

sort of looking forward to it. But mostly I just dread what's going to happen. Too bad it's the only plan we've been able to come up with."

"Yeah. Still, I wish Lugo would decide to leave on his own," Harry said. "Then we could go back to how we used to be."

"Well, he's not going anywhere. So here goes. Phase one of the plan." Monica pulled out a fluorescent-patterned sleeveless unitard and waved it in the air.

Harry laughed. "That's going to be worth three demerits all by itself," she said, heading out the locker room door. "See you out there."

"I'll be right with you," Monica said.

"Today I'll be working with the Gold Stars," Susan Lu explained to the Silvers. "So you guys will have Lugo. As you know, Emma and Dimitri are taking a well-deserved day off." With a quick smile at the Silver Stars, Susan headed to where the Golds were warming up on the floor mats.

"Come, girls," Lugo said briskly, rubbing his hands together. "Today we will work on your saltos on the balance beam."

"We need to warm up first," Kathryn said.

Lugo rolled his eyes. "Five minutes." He held up his right hand, fingers outstretched. "Five. No more." Just then he caught sight of Monica in her Day-Glo outfit. He frowned. Monica tried to look innocent, as if she had simply forgotten they weren't supposed to wear "unprofessional" outfits.

Lugo picked up his clipboard. "One demerit," he said coldly as he wrote it down.

Monica sighed, then turned to wink at Kelly. They had begun to carry out their plan.

For the rest of class, the Silver Stars gave Lugo nothing but grief.

When Lugo ordered them over to the balance beam, Monica skipped there. Candace pretended to chase Kathryn, and Kathryn squealed and ran away. Harry and Maya sang the latest Shanna D. song, and Harry showed Maya how Shanna's new dance steps worked.

Once on the practice beam, however, Monica became all business. It was one thing to goof off while you were waiting your turn, but when you performed, you had to be totally focused. Monica didn't want to risk an injury by not paying attention to what she was doing.

"Use your hands more gracefully," Lugo told her in clipped tones. "Keep your center of gravity low, in your hips. Otherwise you won't have the power to pivot your whole body."

Monica listened to Lugo and tried to do as he said. After her first forward salto, he grimaced.

"Where did you learn this?" he growled. "In a barn?"

Monica could feel her face heating up as though it was on fire. She didn't mind being corrected, but why was he so mean about it?

"No," she said tightly, feeling mortified. "At my first gym, back in New Orleans."

"They were idiots," Lugo said. "Do it again, and this time remember that you are doing gymnastics, not performing in a circus."

Monica gritted her teeth and did the salto again. And again. And again.

Finally Lugo allowed her to get off the beam. When she joined her teammates, Kelly gave her a sympathetic look. One by one the Silvers took their turns on the beam. But while one was performing, the others were going out of their way to earn demerits.

Kelly got two for talking about a television show she had watched the night before. Maya got one for pretending to hurt her knee. Candace got two for tickling Harry until Harry collapsed into a small, giggling ball on the floor.

Then Monica went to get a drink of water without asking permission. When she got back, Lugo snapped, "One demerit."

Monica pretended to count on her fingers.

"That means I have five now," she said, her eyes wide and innocent. "Should I start running?"

For a moment Lugo looked absolutely blank. "No," he said harshly. "Demerits start fresh every day. See, I am very easy on you."

Inwardly Monica sighed. How much worse could she be? She had already done all the outrageous things she could think of. If she did anything *too* obvious, Susan Lu would be sure to notice and might tell Emma and Dimitri.

"He has to be easy on them," Julie Stiller said to Randi Marshall, just loudly enough for Monica to hear. "They can't hack it if he isn't."

Monica bristled as Randi laughed.

"They should be called the Silver Babies, instead of the Silver Stars," Randi said. Julie's irritating laugh floated across the gym, and Monica gritted her teeth.

Looking over at Kelly, she saw that Kelly had heard too. Instantly Kelly leaned over and picked up a damp, sweaty towel. As Monica gasped in horror, Kelly flung it hard toward Julie, catching her right in the face.

"Oh, gross, gross!" Julie screamed, scrabbling at her face to get the towel off.

Susan Lu's head pivoted to see what the problem was, and Lugo stopped dead in the middle of his instructions to Harry.

Monica couldn't help it. Monica began to giggle, then to chuckle, then to laugh out loud. The expression on Julie's face was something to be relished. One by one the Silvers joined in, until they were all laughing uncontrollably, hooting and pointing at Julie, whose face had turned red with fury.

"That does it!" Lugo snapped. "You each have five demerits. Start running! Twenty times around the gym. And your essays will be due on Tuesday. Explain on paper why you are wasting everyone's time and sabotaging your gymnastics career. Now, move!"

He clapped his hands hard, looking angrier than Monica had ever seen him.

Lugo hadn't tried to kick everyone off the Silvers, and so Emma and Dimitri weren't going to notice that something was wrong. All they had accomplished was being forced to run laps and write two-page essays.

So much for our brilliant plan, Monica thought as she started jogging around the perimeter of the gym.

Chapter Fourteen

"Let me guess," Kelly said later that afternoon. She was fixing lunch for herself and Maya, back home in their kitchen. "You want peanut butter on your sandwich."

"No!" Maya cried, looking up in horror. As much as Maya tried to fit in with her American friends and her American family, there were some things that would always be foreign to her. Peanut butter was one of them. Absolutely the only way she could eat the stuff was if it was part of a peanut-butter-and-vanilla-swirl ice cream cone.

Kelly was laughing. "Just kidding. How about tuna salad sandwiches?"

"Much better." Maya nodded. "I'll get the glasses. You want juice or milk or water?"

"Juice, please," Kelly responded.

"Will Emma want lunch?" Maya asked.

"She said she would get it herself," Kelly said. "I think she's upstairs, watching TV in her room. Olympics, of course."

"What's on?" Maya asked, taking a bite of her sandwich.

Kelly frowned. "Shot-putting, I think. A total yawn."

The phone rang. "I'll get it," Maya said. She picked up the wall phone in time to hear that Emma had picked it up upstairs.

"I understand, Doctor," Emma was saying.

"Yes, you only have six months left," a woman's voice said.

"That seems like such a short time," Emma said. "I have so much to get done."

"Don't do too much," the doctor cautioned her. "You have to take care of yourself."

Right then Maya realized that she was listening in and quickly hung up the phone. She stood there, trying to absorb what she'd just heard.

"Maya, what is it?" Kelly asked, coming over to stand next to her. "You look white as a sheet."

"My sheets are pink," Maya murmured.

"Just tell me what's wrong," Kelly said.

Maya looked up at her stepsister. "Kelly, I don't know how to tell you this. That was the doctor on the phone. She was telling Emma that she had only six months left. And Emma said that she had so much to get done in that time."

Kelly sat down hard on a kitchen chair. She looked shocked, as shocked as Maya felt.

"Maybe you didn't understand what they were saying," she said slowly.

Maya shrugged. "I just told you what I heard. We have to ask Papa what's going on."

"Yeah, we do," Kelly said. "But we have to wait for a good time. You know how distracted they've been lately."

"Oh, Kelly, you don't think—" Maya couldn't bring herself to say it.

"No," Kelly said firmly, getting up and going back to her sandwich-making. "No, I don't think that. Absolutely not. For one thing, Mom and Dimitri have been really happy lately, even if they *have* been acting weird. It must be something else. There must be a simple explanation." Kelly slapped some tuna salad onto a piece of bread and spread it around furiously.

"Yes, you're probably right," Maya said doubtfully. "In the meantime, let's both be extra nice to your mom. Maybe when they see we're concerned, they'll tell us what's going on."

"Okay," Kelly said, bringing a sandwich over to Maya. "We'll just help out as much as possible."

"Right."

"More lemonade, Mom?" Kelly held the tall, frosty glass out to her mother. Emma was relaxing in the hammock on the upstairs porch, a pillow tucked under her head.

"Why, thank you, sweetie," Emma said, looking surprised. She took the glass and had a sip. "Delicious. What's gotten into you two today?"

"What do you mean?" Kelly asked. She fluffed another pillow and eased it behind Emma's head.

Emma's eyes narrowed. "Are you in trouble at school?"

"Mom!" Kelly exclaimed indignantly. "No! Geez. Can't someone do something nice for someone without the other one getting all suspicious?"

Emma took a sip of her lemonade. "Well, why is everyone treating me like glass? Maya wouldn't let me carry the laundry upstairs, you're bringing me lemonade. . . . I'm not complaining, mind you, but it does seem unusual."

"Aren't we usually nice to you?" Kelly demanded.

"Yes, of course," Emma said with a laugh. "I guess you're just being extra nice. But I'm not a fragile eggshell, you know. You don't need to wait on me."

Suddenly Kelly felt as if she had to choke back a sob. That was her mother for you—brave no matter what. She knew Emma was just putting on a strong act. But there was obviously something wrong. Why else would Emma have taken the day off?

"Sure, Mom," Kelly said, making sure her voice didn't waver. "Just let me know if you need anything, okay?"

"Will do."

Chapter Fifteen

"Here goes nothing," Kelly said, taking her essay out of her backpack. It was Tuesday afternoon, and class was about to start at SGA. As Lugo had instructed, each Silver Star had written a paper on why she was deliberately sabotaging her gymnastic career.

"This is so stupid," Harry fumed. "What does he expect us to say? Of course we're going to make up a bunch of nonsense."

"It serves him right," Monica said. "Emma and Dimitri would never make us do something like this."

"Let's just get this over with," Kathryn said, grabbing her own essay and heading out the locker room door.

Kelly followed right behind her. She was grateful that at least all of her friends were toughing it out together. With a sigh, she headed out into the main room of the gym.

Lugo Bigue was waiting for the Silvers impatiently. They had deliberately taken as long as they could to change in the locker room, and now they were several minutes late. Frowning, he checked their names off his roll list one by one. Then he put his clipboard down.

Hands on his hips, he glared at each Silver Star in turn. "You are late. You have started the day by earning one demerit. Now, where are your essays?" he demanded.

Wordlessly each Silver Star held out a sheet of paper. If Lugo was surprised that they had actually written the essays, he didn't show it.

"While I read them aloud, you may warm up," he said, tapping the papers into a neat pile. "Perhaps hearing your written apologies will put you into the correct attitude for class."

Kelly sat on the floor and spread her feet wide for some stretching exercises. It was all she could do not to roll her eyes. If Lugo was expecting written apologies, he had another think coming! On Sunday the girls had gotten together and written the most outrageous essays they could think of. It had been hilarious at the time, but now, glancing around at her teammates, Kelly could tell that they were probably having second thoughts. Just like her.

Lugo held up the first paper and cleared his throat.

He's not really going to read them aloud, is he? Kelly thought in alarm. She had pictured Lugo reading them in the office, after class. If he read them now, he'd probably get mad. If he got mad, the rest of the class was going to be more grueling than ever.

"This is by Candace," Lugo said, holding up her paper. " 'The reason I'm sabotaging my gymnastics career,' " he read, " 'is that I might become incredibly famous if I win the gold at the Olympics, and success might go to my head and make me obnoxious, and then I would lose all my friends, and if I lost all my friends I'd probably become bitter and end up a lonely, rich recluse somewhere. So I figure it's best not to get too good now.' "

He put the paper down and looked at Candace. Kelly ducked her head, trying to touch her forehead to her knees.

"Trust me, Candace," Lugo said. "You will never be in danger of winning the gold medal at the Olympics. Rest assured that is one future you do not have to worry about."

Glancing to the side, Kelly saw a red flush creep up Candace's face.

"Ah. This essay is by Kelly Reynolds," Lugo said next. "Daughter of the famous Emma Stanton."

Kelly groaned inwardly. She wondered what her mom and Dimitri would say if *she* wanted to switch to another gym. Right this second, it seemed like a really good idea.

" 'I'm sabotaging my gymnastics career,' " Lugo read, " 'because I might want to be a fashion model when I grow up.' " He looked down at Kelly on the floor. "Kelly, I hesitate to point this out, but you're only four feet, ten inches tall. You're short even for a twelve-year-old. Your dream of being a fashion model is just a little more laughable than your dream of being a successful gymnast."

Kelly pressed her lips together angrily. How dare he say that she couldn't be a successful gymnast? That was what she had been working toward practically her whole life. But more than that, how dare he make fun of how tall she was? "I'm not short," Kelly snapped. "I'm just—vertically challenged."

Lugo threw down the rest of the essays. "I won't waste my time on these," he said. "Do you think I don't know what you're doing? I have been coaching gymnasts since before any of you were born. Never have I seen such a motley bunch as you. But your bad behavior will not be tolerated." He put his hands on his hips and stalked up and down in a tight line. "I am not here to play games with you," he continued. "I am here to teach you to be perfect machines. To perform your gymnastics the best you possibly can, and to be seriously competitive in one of the most competitive sports there is."

He turned to glare at them. "You are wasting my time with your babyish games. I am very expensive. I am costing Emma and Dimitri a great deal of money. So you are wasting their money as well. So now you six have to decide: If you want to come to this gym, you must be willing to do whatever it takes to be number one. Are you serious about your gymnastics or not? If you are, then stay and shape up. If you are not, if you are doing this for fun, or to meet boys, or because you think the leotards are cute, then get out. I have no time for you. If you want to be a winner, then stay. That's all. You decide. Now take a water break. If you're here after the water break, I will assume you want to work. If not, then good-bye."

Looking angry, he strode toward the front office, pausing only to say an encouraging word to Julie Stiller, who was working with Susan Lu on the vault. She smiled and nodded at him.

"Let's get some water," Kelly managed to say weakly.

"I can't argue with what he says," Kathryn admitted in a low voice when they were standing by the water fountain. "It's just that when it comes down to his actually teaching a class, it suddenly seems completely different. I agree that we need to be serious and work hard. And I would like to be a winner, whatever that means. But there's more to it than that."

"Yes," Maya said softly, glancing over her shoulder to make sure they wouldn't be overheard. "I want to be a winner too, but with Lugo you're either absolutely the best or you're less than nothing. But there are lots of other levels. If we were already Gold Stars and had to decide about what level of competition we were going for, that would be one thing."

"Maya's right," Candace said. "Maybe we shouldn't give him a hard time. Maybe we were wrong to do that. But he's wrong too, in how he treats us."

"I don't know what to think," Monica said with a sigh. "All I know is I don't want him to make me quit. I don't want him to win. This plan didn't work, though it was a good idea, Kel. So what do we do now?"

"I don't know," Kelly said slowly. "I guess for now we have to go back to class and do as he says. I just don't see any other way."

Chapter Sixteen

Maya chalked her hands and patted them together to get rid of the excess. Emma was standing to one side of the vault, ready to spot her as she tried a Yerchenko mount.

It was Thursday, and Emma and Dimitri had decided that Lugo would begin class by working with the Gold Stars. Knowing that Emma would be coaching her made Maya feel calm, focused, and determined. It was a nice change from the way Lugo usually made her feel. Wednesday hadn't gone much better than Tuesday had. Maya and the others had tried twice as hard as usual, but Lugo still criticized them as if they were Twinklers. It was very discouraging.

Maya and Kelly still hadn't had a chance to discuss the whole Lugo thing with Emma and Dimitri. Today after school the stepsisters had walked slowly to SGA, dreading yet another afternoon of Lugo's harsh criticism.

"I hate the fact that he usually has a good point," Maya had grumbled. "He *does* know what I'm doing wrong and how to fix it. It's just that he's so mean about it."

Kelly had nodded, swinging her backpack from one shoulder. "I know. When he called me a clumsy moron yesterday, I practically burst into tears."

"Well, Saturday's his last day," Maya had said comfortingly. "Let's get through today, and then we'll have only one more class with Mr. Personality."

Kelly had smiled.

When she found Emma waiting for the Silvers at SGA, Maya perked right up. With Emma coaching her, she would be able to perform much better.

In class Maya was the last one to try her Yerchenko. Starting down at the edge of the floor mats, she ran toward the springboard in front of the vault. At just the right moment, she began her roundoff. Her heels came down hard on the springboard, and she flew through the air in a huge, arching back flip. In a fraction of a second her hands hit the top of the vault, and she pushed off as hard as she could. Once airborne again, she tucked her knees to her chest, then immediately straightened out, her arms out to her sides for balance. The floor mat zoomed into focus. Instinctively she bent her knees to absorb the impact of the landing. And her landing stuck! Proudly she straightened her body, arched her back, and threw her arms overhead.

Emma was smiling. "Excellent, Maya," she said, coming over to pat Maya's shoulder. "You looked great. For a moment I was afraid that you had tucked too late, but you pulled out of it just fine."

For some reason, Maya never minded it when Emma or her father corrected her.

On the sidelines the Silver Stars were cheering and slapping high fives, the way they used to. But their congratulations were interrupted by Dimitri, who stood at the front of the gym and clapped his hands for attention.

"Excuse the interruption," he said. "But may I please see the Silver and Gold Stars here by the offices?"

The Bronze Stars continued to work with Susan Lu as the older students gathered around their head coach.

"What's this about?" Monica whispered to Maya as they waited for Dimitri to speak.

"I don't know," Maya whispered back. "I hope Lugo didn't tell Papa all the things we've been doing." She looked at her father, half afraid, but he seemed cheerful—not angry or disappointed.

"Hello, students," Dimitri said with a smile as Lugo joined him in front of the group. "I just wanted to make a quick announcement. I know you'll be very pleased to hear that Emma and I have made an oral agreement with Lugo Bigue to stay on permanently."

Julie Stiller and some of the other Gold Stars whooped excitedly.

Maya stood there feeling stunned. She looked over at Kelly and saw that her stepsister looked as horrified as she felt.

"We're just waiting for the lawyers to hammer out the details," Dimitri went on. "But I know you'll all benefit from this very experienced coach." He looked around at the Silvers and grinned. "I can tell you're too thrilled to speak. But that's okay. I'm sure Lugo knows how happy you are."

I'm sure he does too, Maya thought in dismay. *That's what I'm worried about.*

Lugo stood there, a broad smile on his face. Most of the Gold Stars, except for Beau Jarrett, were swarming around him, hopping up and down in excitement.

The Silver Stars hadn't said a word. Maya remembered to at least plaster a smile on her face.

"What are we going to do?" she said out of the side of her mouth.

"Maybe we should run away from home," Kelly whispered back.

"Look at him," Monica said quietly in disgust. "He looks like a big blond cat that just swallowed a canary."

"Six little silver canaries," Harry said under her breath.

Maya looked over at Kelly. "We have to talk to Papa again," she said. "We have to try one more time."

Kelly nodded reluctantly. "Let's do it tonight."

That evening, after Maya and Kelly had finished their homework, they went in search of Dimitri.

As Kelly expected, they found him in the small room upstairs that he and Emma had been redecorating. They had moved their home office to the downstairs library, and now this room was empty, except for the ladder and other tools and some painting equipment. Dimitri had repaired the plaster wall he had broken, and then he had painted the walls pale yellow. He was still working on the woodwork, which would be white. The room now looked sunny and clean and much better than the somewhat dingy little office had been.

"Hello, girls," Dimitri said with a smile. "Not glued in front of the TV?"

"Rhythmic gymnastic routines don't start until eight-thirty," Kelly said. "Wow, it looks great in here. So what are y'all going to do with this room?" She and Maya stood in the doorway, looking at everything Dimitri had accomplished. He was up on a ladder, painting the trim around a window.

"Oh, we'll find a use for it," Dimitri said breezily, smoothing the white paint on. He looked down and grinned at the girls. "Perhaps your mother has plans for it."

Kelly looked at Maya. Maya's eyebrows rose, and she shook her head.

"Huh. Well, Dimitri, we wanted to talk to you about Lugo," Kelly said with determination. "Is he really going to stay for good?"

"Yes," Dimitri said. "We just have to work out a few details with his contract. He will be very expensive, but the prestige and publicity he will bring to the gym will be worth it. Also, with another full-time coach, your mother and I can expand SGA. It's been our biggest dream to acquire another building, and more students, and take that final step to becoming a world-class facility."

"I thought you already were," Kelly said, her heart sinking.

"We are in some ways," Dimitri said. "But with Lugo signed on as a full-time coach, we'll be just about the best gym in all of America. That means that Emma and I will have many more opportunities to advance our careers. It's a great thing—our dreams coming true."

Kelly glanced at Maya in despair. "Oh."

"Papa," Maya said, swallowing hard. "We . . . the Silvers, I mean, just don't like him. We think Lugo is too mean."

Dimitri's smile faded, and he turned to look at his daughter. "I'm sorry about that," he said quietly. "Perhaps you will learn to like him as time goes on."

Kelly hoped Dimitri would say more, something encouraging, but he didn't. He just looked at them solemnly.

Maya bit her lip. "Yes, I guess so," she finally said.

Feeling defeated, Kelly turned and left the room, Maya right behind her. "That didn't exactly go as planned," Kelly said.

"No," Maya agreed softly. "Maybe we should talk to Emma."

Sighing, Kelly nodded. "It probably won't do any good, but I guess we might as well. So we can tell the others we tried."

Kelly sneezed. The attic stairs were long, narrow, and dusty.

"Mom? You up there?" she called.

"Yes, right here, sweetie," Emma answered.

Kelly trudged up the stairs with Maya behind her.

"What are you doing up here?" Kelly asked. At the top of the stairs, she saw her mother sitting at one side of the attic, surrounded by cardboard boxes. "You should be taking it easy."

Emma smiled at her. "I'm just sitting here. Not exactly running a marathon."

Maya started looking at some of the open cartons. "What is all this stuff? It looks like . . . old baby stuff."

"Yes, these are all Kelly's baby things," Emma said, pulling out a small pink dress. She lovingly smoothed it over her lap. "You were such a beautiful baby," she told Kelly. Looking up at Maya, Emma grinned. "You might not believe this, but Kelly was a huge, fat baby."

Maya's eyes widened. "*Kelly* was?"

"Yep," Emma said proudly. "She was so plump, with chubby thighs and fat little wrists. Everywhere we went, people exclaimed over her. They thought she looked like a living doll."

Maya giggled behind her hand. "What happened?" she asked.

Emma smiled again. Kelly felt embarrassed that they were talking about her as if she weren't even there. And why was her mom even going through these old boxes? Maybe she was getting all sentimental, reliving old times. Sometimes people who were sick did that.

"She grew up," Emma said, "into the beautiful, graceful, and talented young lady you see before you."

"That's me," Kelly said. Maya shoved her shoulder playfully.

"I always wanted to have another baby, but Kelly's dad and I were divorced when Kelly was barely two," Emma went on. "I saved all this stuff anyway." She pulled out a tiny pair of white shoes, their toes all scuffed.

Maya shot Kelly a meaningful glance.

"Oh, yeah," Kelly said. "Mom, we wanted to talk to you about Lugo—about the announcement Dimitri made today."

"Yes? Are you thrilled that Lugo is signing on permanently?"

"Um, not exactly, Mom," Kelly said. "Actually, we—me and Maya and the rest of the Silvers, I mean—well, we sort of don't like Lugo. He's really—harsh."

"Hmmm." Emma leafed through the pages of Kelly's old baby book. "I'm sorry to hear that. Dimitri and I have been very pleased with his performance so far. I can't tell you how much we've appreciated his help. And we have to think about the future too. If something happened and I couldn't work for a while, think how great it would be for Dimitri to have Lugo to rely on. Susan Lu is a terrific coach, but she's only part-time, since she's going back to school to get her master's." Emma sighed, then smiled at a baby picture of Kelly.

"I'm sorry, girls," she said. "But I'm afraid Lugo's here to stay, and I'm very thankful for it. Maybe you and the other Silvers can try to get along with him for now. Give him another month, and if you're still having problems, come talk to me. We'll see what we can do then, okay?" She looked up and smiled at the two girls.

Kelly could only nod, disappointed. Then she and Maya trooped back downstairs again, where they settled into Maya's room. Kelly leaned back on the bed, right under Maya's Shanna D. poster. Maya flung herself into her beanbag chair, which was her favorite piece of American furniture.

"That's that," Maya said sadly. "He's here to stay, and there's nothing we can do."

"Yeah." Kelly looked up at the ceiling and wiggled her feet. "But I think we might have an even bigger problem."

"What?"

"Did you see what Mom was doing up there? It's like she's looking through her past. Why is she doing that? And did you hear what she said? She said if something happened, and she couldn't work . . ." Kelly swallowed. "What was that about?"

"Gee, I don't know," Maya said, sitting up a little. "I guess I just thought if she had a cold or something."

"No, no," Kelly said in frustration. "Don't you see? This is all tied into everything else—Mom feeling sick, the doctor saying she had only six months . . ."

Maya instantly looked concerned. "You know, Kelly, if your mom is going to start getting sicker and sicker, then it sounds like they really *do* need Lugo. As awful as he is."

Kelly nodded miserably. "I guess we're going to end up being the only two Silver Stars left in a couple weeks. But we have to think of Mom and Dimitri. They really need him, so we can't try to get rid of him somehow."

"Yeah," Maya agreed. "There's just one thing: What are we going to tell the other Silvers?"

Chapter Seventeen

"I never thought I'd say this," Harry said on Friday at lunch. "But I'm glad today is Friday, because we don't have to go to SGA."

"I'm always glad it's Friday," Candace said, taking a bite of her school-lunch pizza.

"Then I'm *extra* glad it's Friday," Harry said.

"I know what you mean," Kathryn said, opening her lunch bag. She pulled out a Thermos of soup and unscrewed the lid. "Lately SGA has stood for Super Glum and Awful. Sorry, Kelly. Sorry, Maya."

Kelly sighed. "It's not our fault. But we told you what Mom and Dimitri said. We really tried, y'all."

"It's okay," Monica said. "We know you did. Let's just do what Emma said: We'll give Lugo another month. If he's still being rotten, then . . . well, I guess I might look for another gym, or maybe just focus on the vet's."

Kelly sighed again. "Maybe I'll come work with you at Fur, Feather, and Scale," she told Monica. "I could help you bathe animals, and feed them, and clean their pens . . ."

The other Silvers started laughing.

"Sure, Kelly," Monica said. "Without gymnastics, you'd be totally lost."

Kelly put her head in her hands. "I know, I know," she groaned. "This next month is going to be the longest month of my life. It'll take a miracle to make me feel better."

"Miracles *do* happen," Kathryn said, taking a sip of milk.

"Yeah, but how often?" Harry said dryly.

"It's a beautiful Saturday," Kelly panted as she and Maya rode their bicycles up onto the sidewalk in front of Super Glum and Awful.

"After class, maybe we should go to the park," Maya suggested, brushing a strand of blond hair off her cheek. Her face was flushed with heat, and her forehead glistened with perspiration. Leaning down, she locked her bike to the rack.

Kelly locked hers next to Maya's. "Good idea. We could ask Monica and Harry if they want to come. We could go skating or something. We'll have to do something nice for ourselves, because we know we're going to feel terrible after class."

Kelly pushed open the double glass doors of SGA, her backpack slung over her shoulder. As usual, it was busy and bustling inside. Sam Gordon Andrew was curled up asleep in this week's favorite spot: right in the front window of the gym, in the sun.

"Hi, sweetie," Kelly said, stroking him gently.

He opened one eye and gave a tiny mew, then went back to sleep.

"Lucky cat," Maya muttered.

Kelly nodded in agreement. Then it started to sink in that something was wrong. At the exact same time, she and Maya noticed that students were huddled in little groups around the gym, looking concerned and confused.

Inside the office, Dimitri was yelling into the phone. "What do you mean, this isn't the right number? Can you give the correct number? No, don't put me on hold!"

Kelly took a step closer and peered into Emma's office. Emma, looking harried and upset, was bending over her open file cabinet, riffling through the stacks of files. "Dimitri!" she called. "Look at this! He took this one too!"

Kelly turned to look at Maya, her eyes wide. "What is going on?"

"I don't know," Maya said, "but it looks big."

"Gosh, there y'all are," Harry said, running up

behind them. Candace and Kathryn were right behind her. Harry had changed for class, but not the twins.

"What's going on?" Kelly demanded.

"We don't know," Harry said. "I got here and started to get ready for class, but then I heard Emma and Dimitri yelling. The Golds haven't even started their class."

"Were Papa and Emma yelling at each other?" Maya asked. "Or just yelling in general?"

"Yelling in general," Kathryn said.

"Guys! Why are you standing there?" Monica had just breezed through the double doors. She checked her watch. "We'd better hurry. I think I see a demerit with 'Monica' written all over it." Finally Monica seemed to catch on that all her teammates were looking strange. "What?" she asked. "Do I have poppyseeds on my teeth?"

Kelly shrugged. "There's something weird going on," she explained.

In the background the phone rang. Dimitri grabbed it.

The Silver Stars leaned closer to hear, trying not to be too obvious.

"Hello? Yes, yes. What? You're not serious. I don't believe this. Well, I'm sorry you feel that way. To be frank, I think you're making a mistake." Dimitri hung up the phone, a grim look on his face. "Emma!" he called. "You will not believe this!"

Emma came out of her office and headed into Dimitri's just as Susan Lu rushed through the front doors.

"Susan!" Emma exclaimed, taking both her hands. "Thank you for coming in on such short notice. Could you please get the classes organized and started? I'll explain in a moment."

"Yes, of course," Susan said. She tossed her handbag onto a chair in the office, then came out and clapped her hands.

The Silver Stars and the small group of Gold Stars gathered around her. Kelly didn't see Julie Stiller anywhere. It was unheard of for her to miss a class.

"What's going on?" Randi Marshall asked. "Where's Lugo? Has something happened to him?"

"I don't know," Susan said honestly. "I know that Emma and Dimitri are trying to sort things out. I understand that it will be difficult for you all to concentrate until you know what's going on, but please get into your leotards and start warming up. Golds, I'd like you to work on your dance movements, once you're ready. I'll be over to select music in a few minutes. Silvers," she continued, turning to Kelly and her teammates, "you guys can get in some practice on the trampoline. I'll give you ten minutes to warm up." She pulled her black hair into a ponytail and took off her light warm-up jacket.

The Silver Stars headed to the locker room to change.

"Maybe Lugo's been in an accident," Candace whispered as they scrambled into their workout clothes.

"That would be awful," Monica said seriously. "As much as I don't like him, I don't want him to be hurt."

"Maybe he just has a cold or something," Maya suggested. "That would be great."

"Yeah," Kelly agreed. "Or maybe he has stomach flu and won't come in for a week."

"That would be heaven," Harry said.

"There's no point in talking about it until we know what's going on," Kathryn pointed out. She twisted her dark red hair into a bun and secured it with bobby pins. Then she headed out into the main room.

"She can take the fun out of anything," Candace complained.

"It's true, though," Monica said. "We'd better not joke about it until we know what's happened. It might be really bad news."

Even though Susan Lu had assigned them to the trampoline—one of the easiest and most enjoyable things to do at SGA—it was still hard for the Silver Stars to keep their minds on their work. They were supposed to be practicing tumbling moves—saltos, splits, flips, body twists, and layouts—but Kelly found her gaze practically riveted to the two front offices where Emma and Dimitri were.

At last, after what seemed like an eternity, the two head coaches came out of their offices. They linked hands, and Kelly saw her mother take a deep breath and release it.

"Please, everyone, may we have your attention?" Dimitri called.

When the Silver Stars and the Gold Stars had left what they were doing and grouped around him, Dimitri continued.

"I know this morning has been very hectic, and I apologize. Something unforeseen has happened." He paused and seemed unsure how to continue.

Emma stepped forward. "We might as well come right out and say it. Lugo has left us. Apparently he signed a contract with a gym in California—he was negotiating with them at the same time that we were trying to work something out with him."

"*Whaaat?*" Kelly felt her mouth drop open in shock.

"He has already gone," Dimitri said, his voice practically shaking with anger. "And what is more, he has taken Julie Stiller with him."

Everyone gasped.

"You're kidding," Kelly said.

"No." Emma's mouth was set in a thin line. "Julie has signed on at the same gym as Lugo, where he will be her coach. Her parents have decided to move to California, and they are home with Julie right now, packing."

"This is terrible," Susan Lu said, frowning in disapproval. "He was such a good coach, but this is unforgivable."

"It might even be legally actionable," Dimitri said, "since he had already made a verbal agreement to stay here. We are talking to our lawyers about any recourse we might have."

"In the meantime," Emma said, "we thank the rest of you for your patience and loyalty. I know you're all terribly disappointed not to work with Lugo. But I assure you we'll continue in our search for a fantastic coach who will become part of the SGA family."

"I was going to tell you this today, after class," a voice said from the back of the group.

Kelly turned to see Beau Jarrett step forward.

"Just yesterday Lugo offered me the chance to go to the gym in California too," Beau said. "I told him no. He might be famous for coaching winners, but I think his methods stink! I'm glad he's gone."

"That's right!" Monica burst out, gazing adoringly at Beau. "We didn't like him either!"

Beau looked over at Monica and smiled. Kelly could feel her practically go limp by her side.

"Get a grip, Monica," Kelly whispered.

"I still can't believe it," Harry said. "I didn't like him, but I didn't think there was anything fishy about him."

"We didn't either," Emma said ruefully. "But it's better that we found out now than later."

"Anyway, we didn't need him," Maya said firmly. "I'm glad you'll be looking for someone else. In the meantime, we'll work extra hard so it'll be easier on you. Right, Silvers?"

"Right!" Kelly cried.

"Right!" Candace, Kathryn, Harry, and Monica echoed.

"We'll be number one—without Lugo!" Kathryn said.

"Yay! Silvers forever!" Kelly yelled, slapping Harry's hand. When she looked up at her mother and Dimitri, she saw that they were smiling again.

"Mom," Kelly said later that day when they were all back at home, "I feel as if half of my problems have been solved."

Dimitri and Maya looked up from where they were working on a jigsaw puzzle together. After the excitement at the gym, they had decided to have a cozy family afternoon, just the four of them.

"Half?" Emma asked, looking up from her *Coaching International* magazine.

"Yeah," Kelly said. "Lugo was really a problem for me. Now he's gone—so that's good. And I'm even glad that Julie's gone. But there's still something bothering me."

"What's that honey?"

"Well . . ." Kelly didn't know how to say it, so she decided to blurt it out. "What's wrong with you, Mom? You've been sick, and seeing doctors—why won't you tell us what's going on? Every time we ask, you just say nothing's wrong, but I know that's not true."

For a moment Emma looked surprised; then she laughed and glanced at Dimitri.

"I told you it wouldn't be easy to hide it," she said. He grinned back at her.

"Hide what?" Kelly felt as if she would scream if she didn't find out what was going on.

"We were going to tell you in a few days anyway," Emma said. "We, that is, Dimitri and I, have very special news for you two. We know it's been a hard adjustment for you to become stepsisters. But you've done such a good job. I truly feel that the four of us are a family now, and it's partly because you two have worked so hard to get along."

Kelly glanced over at Maya, but Maya looked as mystified as Kelly felt.

"We hope you feel you can handle another adjustment," Dimitri said, coming to sit beside Emma on the love seat.

"What?" Kelly shrieked. "Tell us."

"You two are each going to be a big sister," Emma said, a happy smile lighting her face. Dimitri took her hand and squeezed it. "Dimitri and I are going to have a baby in about six months. That's why I've been feeling a little sick sometimes, and why we're really trying to get another full-time coach."

"A—A—" Kelly stammered. "A baby!" She hadn't even considered the possibility! How stupid could she be? Of course her mom could have another baby!

"Oh my gosh," Maya breathed, putting her hand to her mouth. "Kelly, we're going to be related to each other. Not just step anymore. We're both going to have the same sister."

"That's true," Emma said cheerfully.

"That's why you're redoing that little room," Kelly said. Everything was starting to make sense.

"Yep," Emma said.

"And why you were getting out Kelly's baby things," Maya added.

"Guilty," Emma said.

A warm flood of happiness flowed through Kelly. Getting up, she ran over to her mother and threw her arms around her.

"Oh, Mom, that's great news!" she cried. "I was so worried, but now I'm so happy. I can't wait till the baby's here!"

Laughing, Emma hugged her back. "I'm glad you're glad, sweetie. I know you two are going to be the best big sisters ever."

Maya ran over and hugged her father tightly. "I'm really glad too, Papa. I hope it's another girl."

"Another girl!" Dimitri pretended to look horrified. "I need a little boy in this family to help balance it out! I'm already surrounded by women!"

Laughing, Kelly opened one arm and included Maya in her hug, and Maya did the same. The whole problem with Lugo seemed tiny compared to this. Kelly knew what was really important: her family. All four—no, five—of them.

Gymnastic Moves and Positions

Aerial: any gymnastic skill that is performed without the hands touching the floor, such as an aerial cartwheel or aerial walkover.

Back handspring: a back flip of the body onto both hands, with both legs following as a pair. The gymnast begins and ends in a standing position.

Back somersault: a backward roll on the floor or beam, with knees in the tucked position. (The aerial version of this move is called a back salto.)

Back walkover: a move made from a back-arch (or bridge) position, bringing one foot, then the other, down toward the front. Similar to a back handspring but using smoother, more controlled movements and moving arms and legs one at a time rather than in pairs.

Cartwheel: an easy move, in which the hands are placed on the ground sideways, one after the other, with each leg following. Arms and legs should be straight.

Front handspring: a forward flip onto both hands, with both legs following as a pair. The gymnast begins and ends in a standing position.

Front hip pullover: a mount used on the uneven parallel bars. The body is supported on the hands, the hips resting on either bar. Usually combined with a hip circle.

Front pike somersault: a forward somersault in which knees are kept straight.

Front or forward somersault: a forward body roll on the floor or beam, with knees in the tucked position. (The aerial form of this move is called a salto.)

Front split: a split in which one leg is forward, one back.

Front walkover: a move made from a front-split handstand position, bringing one foot, then the other, down toward the back. Similar to a front handspring but using smoother, more controlled movements and moving arms and legs one at a time rather than in pairs.

Handstand: a move performed by supporting the body on both hands, with the arms straight and the body vertical.

Hip circle: a move made by circling either bar of the uneven parallel bars with the hips touching the bar. If the hips do not touch the bar, the move is called a clear hip circle.

Layout: extending the body to its full length, usually during an aerial move.

Pike: any move in which the body is bent and the knees are kept straight.

Roundoff: similar to a cartwheel, but with a half twist, and the legs standing together in a pair. The gymnast ends facing the direction she started from.

Salto: a somersault.

Somi-and-a-half: another way of saying one and a half somersaults.

Sticking: refers to a dismount or final move that is performed without taking additional steps.

Straddle: a position in which the gymnast's legs are far apart at each side.

Straddle split: a split with legs out at each side. This move is used in all four women's events.

Straddle swing: a swing movement on the uneven parallel bars in which the legs are extended at each side.

Swedish fall: a move in which a gymnast does a free-fall drop straight onto the ground, with hands shooting out at the last second.

Tuck: a move in which the knees are brought to the chest.

Yerchenko: a mount for the vault, in which the gymnast does a roundoff onto the springboard.

About the Author

Gabrielle Charbonnet was born and raised in New Orleans, where she now lives with her husband, daughter, and two spoiled cats, Rufus and Fidel. She has written several other middle-grade books, as well as numerous books under a pseudonym.

When she was younger she loved gymnastics as much as the Silver Stars do.